# THE
# HIDDEN WITNESS

---

## THOMAS THOMPSON

A WEST CUMBERLAND MURDER STORY
set in
### CLEATOR MOOR
in the 1820's

*Whitehaven:*
MICHAEL MOON
1999

This tale was originally published in serial form
in the
*Carlisle Express and Examiner*.


First published in book form
by
Isaac Evening, Cockermouth,
in 1872.


Republished in larger format
by
Michael Moon at his Bookshop
19, Lowther Street, Whitehaven, Cumbria
November 1999.


ISBN 0904131 60 2

Cover illustration:
*Ennerdale Broad-water* by **Rev. Joseph Wilkinson**
Published January 1st 1810 by Rudolph Ackerman, London.

TO

## WILLIAM LANCASTER ALEXANDER, Esq.,

OF

Shatton Lodge, near Cockermouth,

THIS WORK IS

# DEDICATED

As a slight Mark of the Respect which is felt for Him by

THE AUTHOR.

# PREFACE.

—:-o-:—

THE following Tale was originally published piecemeal in the
*Carlisle Express and Examiner*, and on its appearance created
an interest and obtained a circulation which surprised no one more
than it did myself. I attribute its success in and around this
locality, not to the intrinsic merit of the Story itself, but to the
fact that the places referred to in it are familiar to every inhabi-
tant of the western division of the county. Indeed, if I am to
believe all that I bear, there are individuals to be found who not
only possess a knowledge of the places, but also of some of the
characters introduced to the notice of the reader. For when the
story was drawing to a close in the columns of the newspaper
already mentioned, I was gravely assured by a lady that a friend
of hers was personally acquainted with Richard Somerville and his
wife and daughter. This statement, I confess, rather startled me
when I heard it; and my readers may, if they choose, accept it as
evidence that "THE HIDDEN WITNESS" is not altogether a work
of fiction.

In the pages which follow I have endeavoured, to the best of my
ability, not only to amuse but to instruct the reader; and in Robert
Fenwood I have tried to depict a man, who, whilst making an open
profession of religion, is at heart a scoundrel of the deepest dye.

That such men are to be found amongst us—that they live, move, and breathe in our midst—no one possessing the slightest acquaintance with mankind will, I think, attempt to deny; and I hold it to be the imperative duty of a public writer to tear the mask off hypocrisy wherever he finds it, and hold it up to scorn and execration. He who strives to maintain religion pure and undefiled, will best discharge his obligations to Society and to God; and one way to so maintain it is to try and prevent its profession from being made a cloak to cover rascality and wickedness of the most abominable kind. Robert Fenwood is, to a certain extent, not the representative of an individual, but of a class, and the sooner that class can be stamped out of existence the better it will be for the world at large.

I may here state that the Tale of "THE HIDDEN WITNESS" was suggested by an incident which I heard related by the late Mr. John Askew, of Brigham. It was my good fortune to make the acquaintance of Mr. Askew in the summer of 1858. A short time previous to that he had returned from Australia, and had published a graphic account of his travels and adventures in a volume entitled "A Voyage to Australia and New Zealand." Mr. Askew possessed a great fund of local and general information, and was gifted with an ability which, if it had had a fair field for its exercise, would have won for him considerable fame. He was one of the kindest-hearted and most unassuming men I ever knew; and his death at a comparatively early age, when the last sheets of his interesting "Guide to Cockermouth," were passing through the press, was deeply lamented by a wide circle of friends. To him, and to my dear and valued friend Mr. William Smith, the proprietor and Editor of the *Whitehaven Herald*, I owe my connection with literature.

I cannot close this Introduction better than by giving a quotation from a letter addressed by Mr. Thomas Carlyle to Colonel Richardson, the author of a work entitled "Literary Leaves; or Prose and Verse," published at Calcutta, in 1836. The author of "Sartor Resartus," referring to the labour of the writer who aims to do good in his day and generation, says :—"He needs, as indeed all men do, the *faith* that this world is built not on falsehood and jargon, but on truth and reason ; that no good thing done by any creature of God was, is, or ever can be *lost*, but will verily do the service appointed for it, and be found among the general sum-total, and all of things after long times, nay after all time, and through eternity itself. Let him 'cast his bread upon the waters,' therefore, cheerful of heart; 'he will find it after many days.'"

*Mountain View, Cockermouth,*
*May 29th, 1872.*

# CHAPTER I.

—o—

*" Seems he a dove? his feathers are but borrowed,*
*For he's disposed as is the hateful raven.*
*Is he a lamb? his skin is surely lent him,*
*For he's inclined as are the ravenous wolves,*
*Which cannot steal a shape but means deceit?"*

*Shakspeare.*

THE extensive and thickly-populated district which
lies some three or four miles to the south of
Whitehaven, and is known by the name of Cleator
Moor, presented a very different appearance about
fifty years ago to what it does at present. The most of
the large and rich fields of mineral, which have proved
sources of great wealth to their owners, and furnished well-
paid and constant employment to hundreds of labourers,
were then quite unknown. The country was sparsely
populated, and instead of the houses forming continuous
rows, as they do now, they were scattered in small groups
here and there, and consisted chiefly of dwellings inhabited
by miners. There were at a considerable distance apart
some buildings of the better class, tenanted by farmers
and persons whose position in life was superior to that of
the labouring population around them, but the number of
such houses was only small. The general aspect of the
country was wild and dreary, and presented but few
attractive features to the lover of the beautiful in nature.

A solitary house, larger than the dwellings of the ordinary workmen in the neighbourhood, was the residence of

B

Robert Fenwood, who occupied the post of manager of one of the collieries on Cleator Moor. He was a native of Northumberland, and spoke with the burr of his native county. Tall, spare, and strongly built, his large hands, long arms, upon which the veins stood out like whipcord, and broad shoulders, indicated the possession of great physical strength by their owner. The face, however, although there was nothing repulsive about it, was not a pleasant one to look at. The features were regularly formed and even handsome, with the exception of the eyes, which were too near each other, and perpetually wandered from one object to another. This shifting, restless expression was certainly not calculated to impress an observer favourably, and a person skilled in reading faces would unhesitatingly have come to the conclusion that Robert Fenwood was not a man to be trusted.

He was a man, nevertheless, who stood well in the estimation of his employers, and in that of many respectable persons resident in the district. He was a professedly religious man, and a prominent and active member of the dissenting denomination to which he belonged, and in connection with which he was what is termed " a local preacher." But there was a wide difference between the Christianity professed by Robert Fenwood and that inculcated by the Great Teacher, whose life was as pure and holy as it was useful, and who went about doing good. The gloomy bigot, who in a harsh voice and coarse language tried to terrify the people whom he was in the habit of addressing by grotesque and horrible descriptions of the last judgment, and the never-ending misery of perdition, knew nothing of the charity which " suffereth long and is kind," and which "thinketh no evil." His was the creed which teaches that innocent enjoyment is sinful; that man is to pass through this world—the work of an all-wise and loving Creator—without turning aside for a single moment to admire its beauties; and that sorrow, and sorrow only, is intended to be the portion of the whole human race. It is almost needless to add that the religion professed by Fenwood was only a flimsy veil, and covered strong passions, which their possessor managed, however, except on very rare occasions, to keep under complete control,

With some of the persons by whom he was surrounded the colliery manager was a great favourite. He was not exactly, they said, the most pleasant and agreeable man in the world; he was harsh and stern; but he was never known to connive at or sanction anything wrong. The men under his control, it is true, had little to say in his praise, but what of that? They were, generally speaking, vulgar, uneducated, drunken boors, whose good or bad opinion amounted to very little indeed, and who required a strong hand to restrain them and keep them in subjection.

Robert Fenwood was unmarried; and his housekeeper was an elderly woman extremely hard of hearing. The inhabitants of Cleator Moor knew as little about her history as they did concerning that of her master, for she was a stranger amongst them, and her residence in the wild district scarcely dated as far back as that of Fenwood himself. By the ladies generally the colliery manager was not much admired. He was entirely, or pretended to be, insensible to the charms of female beauty, and the

very last offence that a woman, especially a young one, is
likely to forgive, is indifference to her personal attractions.
There were some of them with whom he was brought into
contact who read clearly the true character of the man in
his face, and shrank with dread from him as if he were a
leper. But others, possessing intellects less clear and
penetrating, saw only in Fenwood a young and handsome
man, who would make a good match, and great was their
indignation at the coldness and contempt with which he
regarded them.

Amongst the number of those who were favourably
impressed by the colliery manager was Richard Somerville,
a substantial farmer who resided near Wath Brow, and
a member of the same religious body as Fenwood.
Richard Somerville was a man who had passed the prime
of life, but who was strong, hale, and active at the time
he is introduced to the reader—a man with whom time
had dealt gently, whose means were sufficient to enable
him to live comfortably, and whose wants were easily
satisfied. His mode of life was strictly in accordance with
his profession ; he was a sincere and earnest man, whose
religious convictions were deeply rooted, and whose heart
was full of the milk of human kindness. Plain, simple,
and unaffected, Richard Somerville was of the number of
those who lack the power of thinking deeply, and have
great difficulty in separating the true from the false.
Consequently, he saw only in Robert Fenwood a person
whose quiet life and religious enthusiasm entitled him to
respect.

The wife of the farmer was one of those good-tempered
hearty, wholesome-looking women with which Cumberland

—my blessing upon the dear old county!—abounds. The pair had only one child, a daughter, who at the time my story opens had just passed her twentieth year. Mary Somerville was the idol of her parents, who had, to their credit be it recorded, spared no pains in order to give her an education very much superior to that usually possessed by young women in her rank of life. She was extremely beautiful, and her beauty was exactly of that kind which is calculated to produce an impression upon the young and susceptible of the opposite sex. There was a charm about her fair, pleasant face, and winning smile, which had won for her plenty of admirers. Her heart, however, remained untouched until she became acquainted with James Blaylock, a young man who was employed as a clerk at a colliery near to that of which Robert Fenwood had the management. Strong, brave, and handsome, of a frank and fearless disposition, and generous to a fault, James Blaylock succeeded in winning the love, almost before she was aware of it, of the farmer's daughter. But the discovery of her feeling with regard to him produced very little change in the conduct of Mary Somerville. She was a spoiled child, and a coquette. She had been petted by her parents and praised by her admirers until she had reached that state when it is almost impossible for a young woman to live without flattery and homage. The love which James Blaylock felt for her was, it was plain, sincere, and deep-seated; but she could not, for the life of her, make up her mind to turn a deaf ear to the silly talk of the sentimental youths who occasionally tugged wildly at their hair, lauded her loveliness to the skies, and expressed their readiness to die for her sake.

She had no intention of doing wrong, but she could not
resist the temptation of making a conquest whenever it
was possible. Strange to say, this improper conduct—
for improper it was — had never been checked by her
parents. The only person who had ever seriously remon-
strated with her about it was Blaylock himself, and he
noticed with pain that a disposition naturally good and
kind was fast being changed by meaningless and empty
flattery. But his remonstrances were treated with contempt or met with ridicule, and at last he began seriously
to reflect whether it would not be wise on his part to
try and uproot the affection which he felt for a woman
who was giddy and thoughtless, and evidently knew not
what constancy meant.

Matters were in this state when, in the company of her
father, Robert Fenwood for the first time visited the farm
house. Mary Somerville, after she was introduced to the
visitor, mentally decided that he was not by any means a
bad-looking man, but that his voice had a very unpleasant
sound, and was certainly not at all improved by the
Northumbrian burr. Was he a married man, she wondered? Married or single, he was evidently a brute, for
after their first introduction he paid no more attention to
her than if she had been an old Dutch clock. He never
spoke to her, never even looked at her, but talked only to
her father, to whom he spoke in highly eulogistic terms
of a certain preacher who, during the delivery of his
sermons, was in the habit of roaring like a bull, and
trying to knock the pulpit in which he stood to pieces with
the Bible and his fists. Ah! a religious man, thought
Mary; but surely his religion need not have swallowed

up his good manners and left him a churl, totally indifferent to female beauty.

It was Sunday evening, in the summer time, when Robert Fenwood and the farmer and his wife and daughter sat together in the parlour of the old farm house, the two first conversing earnestly about religious matters, the third listening attentively to what was being said, and the fourth eyeing the visitor with a curious and puzzled look. The evening was a lovely one, and the prospect, as seen from the window of the room, was not without its attractive features. The sun was sinking in the west gloriously; not a breath of wind was stirring, and from bush and tree the birds sang merrily. It was a quiet hour—an hour at which a feeling of peace steals over the troubled heart, and the weary wanderer over the thorny and rugged road of life longs for the repose which is only to be found in that happy land beyond the skies.

The two men conversed earnestly for a long time, and at last Robert Fenwood rose to depart.

" Ye're nut gahn to leave us noo, surely?" said the farmer to his visitor. " Stop and hev a bite o' supper."

" Thank you," replied Fenwood, " but I must not remain any longer. The time has gone fast since I came here, and when I get home it will be quite dark."

" Well, what about that?" inquired the farmer. " Surely ye're nut freeten't o' walkin' be yersel' in t' dark, and ye hevn't far to gang."

"I am afraid of nothing," hastily retorted Fenwood, " and if I consulted my own inclination merely, I should accept your kind invitation ; but my housekeeper will be anxious about me, for I am not in the habit of remaining out late. Good night."

"Well, if yé will gang, yé will gang," said the farmer, grasping the hand heartily which was held out to him. "Gud neet, Misther Fenwood, and mind ye caw and see me wheniver yé've a bit o' spare time on yér hands. Yé'll allus be welcome."

Robert Fenwood, having shaken hands with the farmer and his wife, turned to Mary, and fixed his eyes upon her. Her fearless look met his, and in a moment he averted his gaze. Then, with a muttered "good night," he at once turned and left the room. In a short time afterwards, the inmates of the parlour saw him walking rapidly along the road which led in the direction of his home.

"Father, who is that man?" said Mary, pointing to the fast receding figure."

"That's Misther Fenwood," replied the farmer.

"Yes, I know; I heard you call him that. But what is he, where does he come from, and where does he live?"

"Theer's nowt so queer as fwok," muttered Richard Somerville; "and if yé want to git hold o' sumbody 'at 'll inquire a pig's tail out o' joint, yé mun luk out for a woman. What is he? He's t' manager o' Misther Ratcliffe's cwoal pit. Wor does he come fray? Sumway aboot Newcastle side. Wor does he leeve? In a hoose 'at stands be itsel' a lal bit afooar yé cum till t' Innerdale road. Noo, than, is theer owt mair thoo wants to know aboot him? Hes te' tyan a fancy till him?"

"A fancy!" disdainfully repeated the young woman.

"Ay, a fancy," said her father. "Thoo needn't turn up the' nose, me lass, for he's quite a different chap to them bits o' scrafflin' creeturs 'at thoo hes runnin' efter the' sumtimes. Theer's sum on them that luks as if they'd cum't oot o' their graves, and cuddent fin' t' way back agean." And the farmer chuckled with delight at his own wit.

"He's a nice stiddy fellow is Robert Fenwood," the farmer resumed. "He hes neay nonsense aboot him. Gangs till t' chapel regularly, and to be nobbet a local preacher, he's yan o' t' best that iver I listened till in me life."

"A preacher!" said Mary.

"Ay," replied the farmer, "an' a gud 'un. Theer's neay mistak aboot that, hooiver. An' we want sum gud 'uns here, for seck a stiff-necked generation o' vipers as theer is on Cleator Moor it wadden't be possable to fin' any spot else. He preached in our oan chapel to-day for t' furst time sen he com' here, and I nobbet wish thee and the' mudder hed been theer to h'ard him. It was a treat! He nearly flay't old Peggy Setterthet out of her senses."

"And that you consider good preaching?" said Mary.

"To be sure," replied her father. "We want sumbody that 'll stir sinners like her up, t' seame as a man in a menagerie stirs up a lot o' wild beasts. But I doon't think thoo need bother theesel' aboot him, Mary, me lass. He wants nowt wi neay wimmen."

"I don't intend to bother myself about him!" indignantly answered the young woman.

"Neay," responded her father, "and if thoo was to bother theesel' less wid sum that isn't hawf as gud as him it wad mebbe be better for the'. To tell the' t' truth,

Mary, thoo's far ower leet-heeded. I doon't think thoo means owt wrang—far fray it; but thoo should hev mair sense than thoo hes. If thoo wants a husband, pick out a sensible, stiddy young fellow that 'll mak the' a gud 'un, and be dun wid it; and if thoo duzzent want to hev owt to dee wid a man, doon't lead him to think, be the' ways that thoo's in luv wid him. It isn't reet; it's sinful; and t' suiner thoo turns a fresh leaf ower, me lass, and t' better, beath for the' oan seake and t' seake of iverybody aboot the'. And noo let's hev our suppers, and git off to bed."

The plain speaking of her father went like an arrow to the heart of Mary Somerville, and produced a strange sensation there. Her conscience told her that the accusation made against her was true, and she thought with a pang of regret of the sufferings and pain she had been the means of inflicting upon James Blaylock by her heartless conduct. She made no reply to what her father had said, and ate her supper in silence, but the feeling produced by his words soon wore off, and before the family separated for the night she found herself thinking of Robert Fenwood.

She felt considerably annoyed that her thoughts should run in such a direction. For what was the man to her? Nothing. She had only seen him once, and he had certainly made no attempt to ingratiate himself with her. This was really what provoked her. His insensibility to her charms, his disregard of her presence, the cool, unceremonious manner in which he had treated her, were very galling to her vanity, and made her fume and fret like an irritated school girl.

When she laid down to rest that night, she did so with an unsettled, uneasy mind.

" I am a sad girl," she murmured, " and I am afraid I give great pain sometimes to one of the best and noblest men that ever breathed. But he knows I mean no harm by my foolish conduct ; and he ought to know, if he does not, that my heart beats only for him. I think I will take the advice of my father, and turn over a new leaf. For I am not happy at present, and sometimes I get into such a queer way that I fall out with myself."

With a sigh the speaker turned her face to the wall, and the pillow upon which her head rested soon became wet with her tears.

# CHAPTER II.

—o—

"The thread of our life would be dark, Heaven knows,
  If it were not with friendship and love intertwined,
And I care not how soon I may sink to repose,
  When these blessings shall cease to be dear to my mind.

But they who have loved the fondest, the purest,
  Too often have wept o'er the dream they believed;
And the heart that has slumber'd in friendship securest,
  Is happy indeed if 'twas never deceived."—*Moore*.

THE following morning Mary Somerville rose with an aching head and a disturbed mind, and when she presented herself at the breakfast table, looked so ill as to attract the notice of her mother, who inquired, with the anxiety which only a mother can feel, what it was that ailed her. Nothing, the young woman answered; she had not slept well, and her head ached very much, but she would soon be better.

"Thoo munnet think owt aboot what I said till the' last neet," said her father. "I niver intended to hurt the' feelins. Aw that I want the' to dee is to tak care o' thesel' an' nut try and mak fuils o' fwok. An' if thoo duzzent tak that advice, thoo may depend neay good 'll cum on 't. Theer's somebody at t' door, Ellen," he added, turning to a servant girl who was sitting at the table. "Gang an' see whea it is."

The girl rose from her seat to obey the command, but before she could reach the door which led out of the farm-yard into the kitchen where the family were seated, it opened, and a man walked into the room.

There was something very striking about the appearance of the new comer. He was a tall and powerfully-built man, but his sturdy frame was slightly bent by age, and his hair was whitened by the frosts of nearly seventy winters. His clothes were poor and threadbare, and patched in many places, but they were very clean. The face, bronzed by exposure to all kinds of weather, had a sad and patient look, and its mournful expression was increased by the eyes, wide open and sightless, which the man quickly turned first to one part of the room and then another. In his right hand the new comer carried a stout stick, and in his left a basket containing a quantity of articles which he hawked about the country for sale.

Charles Loftus, "the blind pedlar," as he was commonly called, was well known not only on Cleator Moor, but in every village within ten miles of Whitehaven, where he resided. The trade of a pedlar was at that time much more profitable than it is at present, for the facilities for obtaining goods required for household purposes were not so great then as they are now; and although the stock of articles which the blind man owned was only a small one, he managed not only to make a comfortable living, but, so report said, to save money. He had his regular customers in all the villages which he visited, and by them he was heartily welcomed whenever he called upon them. For the pedlar was an active picker-up of local news; and as newspapers were then scarce and dear, and found their way but rarely into the places around Whitehaven, his visits were as much valued for the stock of local information which he possessed and was always willing to impart, as for the supply of tapes, thread, and needles which he carried about with him. His sense of hearing, like that of most persons deprived of sight, was very acute ; and he could also walk from Whitehaven to every village which he was in the habit of visiting, without the slightest assistance, and return home in safety alone.

Such was the somewhat singular being who stood on the floor of the kitchen in the farm house, turning his blind face to every part of it, as if in search of some one with whom he was acquainted.

" Cum' forret, Charley, said the farmer, " and sit doon. Hoo is te' gitten on, min ? Thoo's suin astir. What's browt the' on t' Moor at this time o' mornin' ? "

The blind man deposited his stick in a corner of the kitchen, and sat down upon a chair which was handed to him before he replied.

" I left Whitehaven very soon," he said, in a voice which was low and musical, and in language unmarked by the county dialect, " because I want to get back home again as fast as I can. My sister, with whom I live, is very poorly."

" Sorry to hear that," said the farmer. " What's t' matter wid her, min ? "

" She has got cold," replied the blind man, " and has been so ill for the last two or three days that she has not been able to stir out of the house."

" Ay ! " exclaimed the farmer, " that's nut so weel. But is theer owt new aboot Whitehebben ? "

"Nothing particular," replied the pedlar. "I suppose you have heard of that coal-pit which took fire last Tuesday?"

"I hev indeed," said Richard Somerville, "and an awful job it seems to hev been."

"Ah, you may well say that," replied Loftus, shaking his head sadly. "I was at home that day, and as soon as I heard what had happened, went straight to the pit top. I have sometimes grieved, Mr. Somerville, over my want of sight, but that day I felt as if it were almost a blessing that I was blind. I could not see them, but I could hear the women and children sobbing, and crying out at intervals, 'Oh, father, where are you?' or else, 'Oh, my poor husband!' And then, as the men were brought up the shaft and gently laid upon the ground, some of them dead, others dying, and the most of them so frightfully burnt—as I learnt from the people standing around me—that it was with difficulty they could be recognised, the cries broke out again louder than ever, until at last they died away in a low sad wail, that would have melted the heart of a stone."

The speaker paused for a moment, and then resumed.

"One of the men, named Jem Slaney, lived next door to me and my sister in Scotch Street. He was only a young man, but he had a wife and five children, and his wife was at the pit top, with the youngest child in her arms, when her husband was brought up the shaft almost burnt to a cinder. As soon as she saw him she gave a shriek that went like an arrow through the brain of everybody who heard it, and fell senseless upon the ground. They took her and her husband home, and he was

attended by a doctor ; but his case was a hopeless one
from the first, although his poor wife kept praying and
hoping that he would get better. For he was a good
husband and a kind father, and tried to do what was
right to everybody about him. On Saturday night, just
as I was thinking about going to bed, his wife came into
our house, and said to me, ' Charley, will you come in
and sit with Jem a little bit ? He's very bad.' ' To be
sure, my lass,' I answered ; and I went into the house
with her. When I got into the room where he was lying,
I could hear the poor fellow breathing heavily, and the
children that were about the bed were trying to stifle their
sobs. ' Is that you, Charley ? ' he said when he saw me.
' It is, my lad,' I answered ; ' how do you feel ? ' ' About
as bad as bad can be,' he replied, in a feeble voice. ' Eh,
Charley, mine has been a poor miserable life. Ever since
I could crawl I have known nothing but hard work, and
this is the end of it. I could bear up against it myself,
for I am not afraid to die ; but oh, Charley, Charley,
what will become of the wife and bairns when I am gone ? '
His voice died away in a whisper, and I was almost distracted by the cries of the children — which they were
unable to keep down when they heard his words—and by
the grief of his wife. When he spoke again, he said,
' Charley, give me your hand ; and Jane,'—that was his
wife—' come and sit down beside me, and take my other
hand, and let me try and fall asleep so.' We both did as
he desired us, and presently his breathing became very
low, until at last it died away altogether. His wife and
I sat quiet for some time for fear of disturbing him, but
suddenly she gave a start, and sprang from her seat with

a cry that I never shall forget till my dying day. For her disfigured and tortured husband had fallen asleep, never to wake again until the Archangel, standing with one foot upon the sea and another upon the land, proclaims that time shall be no longer."

The blind man rose as he uttered the last words in a thrilling tone, but immediately after they were spoken the excitement which had animated him died away, and his face resumed its usual quiet look.

" It's dreadful," said the kind-hearted farmer, much agitated by the narrative to which he had listened, and which had moved his wife and daughter to tears. " God help poor fwok ! Hoo many men hes there been kill't be this fire ? "

" Ten," replied the pedlar. " But the day is getting on, and I must be taking the road again. Mrs. Somerville," he continued, taking the cover off his basket, " do you want anything in my way to-day ? If you don't, I know your daughter does, bless her sweet face ! "

" Dang it, Charley," said the farmer, " thoo sud ha' been a young chap ! I didn't think thoo hed as much in the' as that."

" What do you mean by ' that' ? " inquired the pedlar.

" Wey, blessin' sweet feaces, and buttherin' t' wimmen up. Eh, but thoo's a queer old shaver," said the farmer, with a chuckle.

" I love the women, or rather the ladies," said the blind man, raising his shabby old hat from his head with a dignity that would have done honour to a prince.

" What, ivery yan on them ? " inquired Richard Somerville.

C

" Every one of them," was the reply.

" T' ugly 'uns an' aw ? "

" There never was an ugly woman," gravely responded the pedlar. " For shame, Mr. Somerville. The ladies are our best friends. They cheer us in sorrow, tend us in sickness, and what is more important than anything else, they are my very best customers."

This strange association of ideas tickled the fancy of the farmer amazingly, and the pedlar, who was thoroughly the master of his business, soon succeeded in disposing of a number of articles to Mrs. Somerville and her daughter. When this was done, he rose to depart.

" Thoo hes to gang, than, Charley ?" said the farmer.

" I must indeed," answered the pedlar. " The time flies fast, and I have many weary miles to travel before I turn back again to Whitehaven. Good day to you all."

" Gud day," replied Richard, " and I expect t' next time thoo cums this way that the' sister 'll be better."

" I hope so " answered Loftus ; " but," he added, reverently, " the will of God be done."

As deliberately and as correctly as if he had possessed that sense of which he was totally deprived, the pedlar took his stick out of the corner where he had placed it, lifted his basket, opened the door of the kitchen, made his way straight across the farm yard, passed through the gate, and proceeded at a brisk pace along the road leading to Egremont.

The same evening James Blaylock, the young man for whom Mary Somerville did feel a true and sincere affection, visited her at her father's house. He was a great favourite with the parents of the young woman—indeed, he was a favourite with every one who had the slightest acquaintance with him. The farmer liked him because he was such a manly, sensible young fellow. He "wasn't yan o'thur daft fuils that can admire nowt but their oan legs, and that walks wid their he'ds stuck o' ya side like an old clockin' hen." Mrs. Somerville liked him because, whenever he visited the house, he always found time to spare for a conversation with her about what was going on in the neighbourhood, and his manner towards her was marked by a kindness and consideration seldom to be met with in young men of his class. The relation in which James Blaylock and their daughter stood towards each other was perfectly well understood by Richard and his wife, and both of them sometimes felt pained at the way in which he was treated by Mary. But the farmer, especially, consoled himself with the thought that "young fwok," as he said "wad be young fwok;" that the heart of his daughter was in the right place; that she would soon settle down; and that in a little time all would be well.

James Blaylock remained conversing with the farmer and his wife until the sun went down, and then he rose.

"Will you take a short walk, Mary?" he said, turning to the young woman, who had scarcely opened her lips since he entered the house.

"It is getting late," she answered, coldly.

"Tut!" said her mother, sharply. Hod the' daft tongue, lass. It's nut that leate, and thoo needn't be freeten't; thoo'll see nowt warse than thesel'—varra likely nowt hawf seay bad. Loavins bless us!" she continued, "I wunder what t' warld 's comin' till! When I was a lass, ya sweetheart was plenty for me; noo theer's some that nowt less than hawf-a-dozen 'll sarra; an' if I'd behaved to the' fadder as I see thee behave sumtimes, he wad ha' seen me at t' back-o-beyont afooar he wad ha' hed owt to dun wid me. Put the' hat and shawl on, an' dee as James wants the'."

The young woman rose silently, her pretty face wearing a look of disdain, and complied with the order of her mother. After the young couple had left the house, Mrs. Somerville turned to her husband.

" I'll tell the' what, Richard," she said, " I diven't like t' way that our Mary treats that young fellow at aw. She's far owre fickle-minded, and I begin to think that we're beath on us to bleame for letting her hev far ower much of her oan way."

" I dar say thoo's reet, Betty," replied the farmer, with a sigh ; " but wat can we dee ? I diven't like to begin and be cross wid her. It'll aw cum reet in a lal bit o' time, an' I think theer's varra lal fear of her deein' owt that'll disgrace owder thee or me."

" Mebbe nut," answered his wife ; " but I wish to gudness she was mair settled. That young chap 'll mak her a gud husband if she only hes t' luck to git him ; but that's hardly likely, if she keeps on first lettin' ya clothe'd mak love till her, and thananudder."

Meanwhile the pair who were the subject of this conversation had left the farm house behind them, and were pursuing their way slowly, arm-in-arm, along a road winding round the base of a hill. For a considerable distance they walked together in silence, which was at last broken by the young man.

"Mary" he said " are you offended with me ?"

" No," was the curt reply. " Why do you ask ?"

" I thought you were. You have scarcely spoken to me during the whole evening."

Another long silence, and again James Blaylock spoke.

" Mary," he said, " I cannot bear this suspense any longer, and it is better that you and I should understand each other once for all, so as to prevent mistakes. Listen to me."

He released his hold of her arm, and stood before her in the middle of the road. Her heart beat quickly, and the blood rushed into her countenance, but the colour soon died out, and left her face as white as that of a dead woman.

" Mary Somerville," began the young man, in a low earnest voice, " I love you. If you have noticed my conduct since we became acquainted ; if you feel a thousandth part of the interest in me which I feel in you,—it is needless for me to tell you that I love you. But I do tell you so, nevertheless, and I am uttering no untruth when I say that to save you a moment's pain I would freely lay down my life. Look at me, and tell me if I lie !"

He seized her by the hands as he spoke, and she fixed her eyes upon his face. It was a frank, manly, handsome face she thought, and she felt proud of the avowal which he had made.

" I do not want to say too much about myself " he continued, " or my position. Concerning the first I think I may assert that my character is unstained, and that no one can accuse me of anything about which I need be ashamed. With regard to the second, it is such as will enable me to keep myself and my wife, whoever she may be, in comfortable circumstances. I believe your parents think well of me ; indeed they have no reason to think otherwise. With reference to yourself, sometimes I have imagined that you do care for me, and at other times I have thought differently. I wish to know from you to-night my true position in relation to yourself. For I am not such a simpleton, Mary Somerville, as to allow any woman to play with me as a spoiled child plays with a toy, and then throws it carelessly to one side when it is tired of it."

He paused for a short time, as if to allow her to speak, but she remained silent, and he resumed—

" You are unjust to yourself, Mary : that I see clearly. You strive to keep out of sight the noble qualities which I am convinced you possess. Excuse me for speaking plainly, but it is for your own sake that I do so ; and I tell you that you ought to be above anything like affectation, and you would be above it if you would only let your good and truthful nature have its way."

" What right have you to talk to me in this manner ?" passionately asked the young woman.

" In the strict sense of the terms," he replied, " I have no right, nor do I claim any beyond the right which an affection such as mine gives me to warn you of danger, and to strive to insure your happiness. But, surely a love like mine demands something more in return than that I should be treated as if I were a fool or a child. Mary Somerville, I declare to you, before God, that I love you as truly and as deeply as ever man loved woman ; and I want to know from your own lips now, to-night, if you

23

love me. If you cannot answer me that question with a plain straightforward Yes,—though my heart should break in the struggle, I'll tear your image from it, and part from you at once and forever."

# CHAPTER III.

—o—

"*Sincerity, thou first of virtues,*
*Let no mortal leave thy onward path,*
*Though from the gulf of hell destruction cry*
*To take dissimulation's winding way.*"—*Hume.*

THE plain, straightforward manner of James Blaylock—his evident determination not to suffer himself to be trifled with—took Mary Somerville completely by surprise. She loved him, but she wanted to acknowledge that love in her own way and at her own time. He had no right, surely, to begin and give himself airs, and question her in this manner. If he were as much in love with her as he pretended to be, he would never have done it.

The young woman stood, after James Blaylock had finished speaking, with an expression of mingled vexation and annoyance resting on her beautiful face, but she did not offer to reply.

"I am waiting for your answer, Mary," said the young man, after a long silence.

"What am I to answer?" she inquired, coldly.

"My question."

"What is it?"

"Mary," cried James Blaylock, passionately, "why will you persist in trifling upon a subject which involves the happiness or misery of my whole life? I ask you, do you love me?"

"I don't think you have any right to ask such a question," was the haughty reply."

The young man stared in amazement at the speaker apparently under the impression that he had not heard her aright.

"Besides," she proceeded, "under any circumstances I am not bound to answer it, and certainly don't feel disposed to do so. Come, it is getting late, and I want to return home."

The young man passed his hand across his brow, and his handsome face, white even to the lips, wore a look of intense pain. The coquette noticed that look, and her own heart died away within her. For a moment the impulse was almost irrisistible to yield to her feelings—to throw herself on his breast and tell him how delighted his avowal of love had made her, how dear he was to her, how ready she was to walk the path of life side by side with him. But in another moment the impulse yielded to the false pride which had taken so firm a hold upon her, and her wretched and miserable vanity whispered that the young man would not be able to remain away from her for long, and that at any time she thought proper she could bring him back a suppliant to her feet.

The Creator in his mercy has drawn a veil across the future which conceals it from our eyes. If Mary Somerville could have lifted that veil but for an instant, and seen the terrible results which were to spring out of the part she was playing, she would have gone raving mad.

"Wait but a moment," said James Blaylock, with quivering lips, after he had recovered somewhat from the shock which her rude and heartless speech had given him, "and

I will see you home. May God forgive you Mary Somerville, as freely as I do for the blow which you have dealt me to-night! I will trouble you no more. But the time may come when you will stand in need of a friend to assist you in distress or console you in sorrow, and if ever that time does arrive, rest assured, Mary, that what you have done and said to-night will not prevent me from being that friend."

He offered her his arm, and she took it without saying a word. She could scarcely believe in the reality of what was taking place. Surely James Blaylock was not speaking seriously when he said that they must part for ever that night. Oh, how she longed to tell him that he alone held a place in her heart, and that she had never meant to treat him unkindly! but again the impulse to do right was crushed, and the words of penitence and love which sprang to her lips were forced back, and found no utterance.

They wended their way back to the farm house in silence. The moon had risen, and mountain and moor were bathed in a flood of silver light. Standing out in bold relief stood the solitary old building; and the silence of the night was unbroken by a single sound.

They stopped at the gate leading into the farm yard, and Mary ventured, very timidly, to look up into the face of her companion. It was pale and sad, but not a single trace of passion distorted the noble features. He quietly took her hand.

"Mary," said he, "before I leave you, I ask you to reflect again upon what I have said to-night. Tell me that I am not indifferent to you; tell me if months, ay, even years of patient and unswerving devotion will induce you to look favourably on my suit; tell me that I am something more to you than the mere idlers and fools who are as heartless as they are brainless, and who persuade themselves that they are dying for the love of every woman, and that every woman is dying for the love of them."

She stood silent, and once more her better angel strove for the mastery. But the thought quickly passed through her mind that it would be unpardonable weakness on her part to yield now, and she answered coldly—

"You have my reply, and it is the only one I am disposed to give you."

"Then farewell Mary," he said, hastily. "I will trouble you no more."

He pressed her hand and left her. Yes, he was gone, and she was alone. How bitterly she condemned her own folly, which had induced her to cast from her as a thing of no value one of the noblest hearts that ever beat in the breast of man. She would have given worlds to recall the events of the last half-hour; and as the form of James Blaylock disappeared round a turn of the road, a sense of utter desolation fell upon her, and she sobbed like a child.

She stood leaning against the gate for some time, weeping bitterly. At last she roused herself, opened the gate, and crossing the farm yard, entered the house. Her father was sitting by the fire smoking his pipe; her mother was folding up a pair of stockings which she had been mending; the servants, three in number, had retired to rest. The young woman, as soon as she entered the kitchen, took a candle, bade her parents good night, and went upstairs to her own room, there to think alone of the misery which she had brought upon herself.

The week passed away, and Mary Somerville strove, as well as she could, to bear up against the grief which was oppressing her. The following Sunday evening, Robert Fenwood again visited the farm. He came alone this time, and was received with great cordiality by the farmer and his wife. He shook hands very heartily with them both, but there was an air of awkward embarrassment about him when he turned to greet Mary, and the evil eyes became more shifting and restless than ever.

The conversation which took place was carried on mainly between the farmer and Fenwood; but the part which Richard Somerville took in it was very insignificant indeed. Fenwood mounted his own peculiar religious hobby, and dashed along upon it with amazing vigour. The farmer was content to sit and watch the rapid progress of his friend, occasionally throwing in a word to help him on the way. At last the colliery manager thoroughly exhausted his subject, and then the discourse becoming more general, all present, including even Mary herself, began to take part in it.

She thought within her own mind that Fenwood was one of the strangest men she had ever met with, and wondered if all the religious zeal which he manifested was heartfelt, or a mere sham. Her father had led her to suppose that the visitor was not a man likely to be impressed by womanly beauty, and, so far as she could judge, such appeared to be the case. But, she reasoned, it was possible, by the exercise of those arts and graces which her training in the school of flirtation had taught her, to make the religious enthusiast think very differently to what he appeared to do of women in general, and very much indeed of herself in particular.

For a day or two after her parting with James Blaylock, she had been almost broken-hearted, and bitter and sad were her feelings whenever she thought of him—and that was always. He was ever present before her mind. She tried to persuade herself that he had treated her badly, but her conscience told her that this was a lie. She had believed that after the fit of annoyance, consequent upon her conduct on the night of their separation, left him, he would return to her, ask her pardon, and be to her what, until he had asserted his manhood, she had thought him— an humble, willing, and obedient slave. But a week had almost elapsed, and there was no sign of his return. She had heard of him as following, in his own quiet way, his ordinary employment, but she had never seen him since he left her at the farm-yard gate. Her parents knew of the rupture that had taken place between them, for she had been compelled to state, in order to account for his absence, that they had quarrelled, and she gave an account of the affair as favourable to herself as she could possibly make it. But that version failed to make a good impression upon either her father or her mother, who both censured in severe terms her treatment of the young man, and her light and frivolous conduct. This censure, instead of arousing her to a sense of the impropriety of her own conduct, only added to the indignation which she felt against James Blaylock. It was this indignation, and the love of making a conquest, which led her to form the determination of playing off her graces upon the stern and gloomy colliery manager.

When Robert Fenwood rose to leave the farm house that night, the coquette gave him her hand with a readiness that surprised him. His eyes met hers for a moment, and the look that he saw there sent the blood rushing to his face. Scarcely knowing what he did, with a muttered " Good night," he released her hand quickly, and left the house.

He became a constant and almost nightly visitor at the farm house from that time, and it is almost needless to say that Mary Somerville accomplished her purpose, and that he soon loved her with a passion which natures like his alone can know. If the truth must be told, the young woman, as soon as she saw the effect produced by her acting, became slightly alarmed. When her vanity and annoyance at the conduct of James Blaylock had led her to try the effect of her charms upon Robert Fenwood, she had no conception that the religious enthusiast would become such a devoted lover. He had not ventured, as yet, to make any formal declaration of his affection, and she dreaded his doing so. There still remained in her heart—cold and unfeeling as thoughtlessness and un-checked frivolity had made it—that old passion for the young clerk, and she could not eradicate it. Why did he not return to her, or would he ever return ? Such were the questions she had asked herself, and reasoned blindly that the best way to conquer his indifference, as she thought it, would be, if possible, to arouse his jealousy. She was led to think that when he learnt how intimate were the relations which subsisted between herself and

Robert Fenwood, James Blaylock would come back to her. But in this expectation she was sadly disappointed. He never looked near her. If he heard at all, as probably he had, of what was going on, he never troubled his head about the matter. He treated, or seemed to treat, his former sweetheart with silent contempt, and this to her— so vain, so proud of her beauty—was by far the most galling treatment to which she could have been subjected.

Her parents looked upon everything as at an end between Mary and James Blaylock, and began to regard Robert Fenwood as their future son-in-law. This the young woman saw plainly, and it added to the uneasiness which she was beginning to feel. As for the colliery manager himself, there was a certain amount of pleasurable excitement in leading him on, step by step, to love her, and persuading him, by discarding all the empty-headed simpletons who pretended to be dying for her sake, that she cared for him alone. But she thought with dread of the time when it would become necessary for her to avow that she had only been playing the hypocrite, because she was determined not to marry him. As the time passed, the difficulty of keeping up her assumed character became greater and greater, for the more she saw of Robert Fenwood the less she felt disposed to accept him as a husband. She felt that a storm was gathering, and that it would ere long break over her devoted head.

One evening Richard Somerville and his family, with Robert Fenwood, were sitting in the large old-fashioned kitchen of the farm house, when the conversation in which they were engaged was interrupted by the entrance of a visitor, who certainly presented a somewhat extraordinary appearance. He was a little man, rather lean, and dressed as a labourer. His features were neither very handsome nor very ugly ; but what gave him an odd and somewhat comical appearance was the total absence of eye-lashes and eye-brows from his face. On entering the room he removed the cloth cap which covered his head, and awkwardly saluted the company, revealing at the same time the fact that a considerable quantity of the hair on his head had been destroyed—evidently by fire.

The farmer stared at the new-comer in amazement for a short time, and then burst out laughing.

"Bless my heart, Jimmy," he said, " what hes te' been deein' wid the'sel, min ?"

" Who is the man ?" said Fenwood, turning with a grim smile to Mary, who was laughing as heartily as her father.

" They call him James Jenkins," replied the young woman. " He lives a short distance from here."

" Eh Misther Sumerville " said the visitor, shaking his head mournfully, "sec a job as niver was h'ard tell on. I'll tell yé what it is " he added, with a sudden change from sorrow to ferocity, and bringing his fist down with a bang upon a table which stood near him, " theear's sec a lot o' divils leeves on this Moor as theear isn't in England.

"Wey, what's t' matter, min ?" inquired the farmer. " What hev they been deein' till the' noo ?"

" I'll tell yé " replied Mr. Jenkins. " Yé know wor I leeve ?" The farmer nodded. " My hoose stands at ya side o' t' road, an' old Tim Flanigan's at t' udder. Varra weel. Last neet me and our Nanny was sittin' be t' fire, thinkin' aboot gahn to bed, when sumbody gev a kick at t' dooar as if they meen't to send it off t' hinges.

'Bless me sowl!' ses I to Nanny, 'What's that?' Than theear com anudder girt kick. 'Thoo hawf-witted maizlin', ses Nanny to me, ses she, 'divn't sit theear, but gang an' oppen't dooar!' Well, when I reach't it, theear com anudder girt kick. 'Dang my buttons!' ses I, 'but when I dui git t' dooar oppen I'll wallop the' if iver a fellow was wallop't! Well I got hold o' t' sneck, an' pull't till I was varra nar black in t' feace. While I was pullin', theear com anudder girt kick. 'Oppen t' dooar, thoo fuil!' roars Nanny. 'Divn't caw me a fuil, thoo oald sackless,' ses I, 'but cum ere an' help me. Theear's summat hes hold o' t' dooar.' Git oot wid the'!' ses Nanny; and she com till wor I was. Well, she pull't, and I pull't, and while we wur pullin' I thowt I cud hear old Flanigan roarin' like a bull ower at t' udder side o' t' road. 'What's t' matter wid Tim?' ses I. 'Hoo can I tell?' ses Nanny; an' than theear was anudder girt kick. 'Pull, min!' shouts Nanny; 'pull for the' life!' Sh'd hardly gitten t' words oot of her mooth when t' dooar gev way, an' beath on us went neck an' heels reet intil t' middle o' t' flooar. As suin as I com till mesel'—for I was varra nar knock't daft—I ran ootside an' fund old Flanigan theear screamin' like mad, an' a bit of a brat, aboot twelve or thirteen 'ear old, stannin' wid his hands in his briches-pockets. 'Whea was't at kick't at oor dooar?' ses I till t' lad. 'Sum chaps,' ses he. 'Whea war they? What do they caw them?' ses I. 'Divn't know,' says he. 'Was thoo nut yan on them?' ses I. 'No,' ses he, 'I wasn't.' 'Is te' sure on it?' ses I. 'Ay, I is.' 'Because,' ses I, 'if I thowt thoo was, I wad mak the' think that sumbody had emptied a carfull o' steanes on the' heed. But hoo the

D

divil was it 'at I cuddent git t' dooar oppen?' 'They tied your door and mine together,' ses old Flanigan, fleein' up an' down like a kite widout a tail. 'Than we wur pullin' t' yan agean t' udder,' ses I. 'We wor,' ses he, 'and a sore pullin' it has been to me. There's my wife lying on the broad ov her back on the flure kilt, and I have a lump on the back ov me head the size of a duck egg, from the fall I got. But be the 'tarnal war!' ses he, 'if I can only find the vagibones, I'll chase them to Americay!' Well, I went intil t' hoose, an' left Flanigan in t' road, and efter a bit he went in. I'd hardly got sitten doon be t' fire, when theear com a thunner at t' dooar fit to waken a corp. I bounce't fray me seat an' ron across t' flooar. 'Goyson?' ses I, 'but I'll settle wid you this time.' Just when I gat t' dooar oppen, theear was summat went off wid a bang like a cannon. I flew back; Nanny gev a scream; t' hoose was full o' smook in a minnet: and when I com to luik at mesel' I fund that me eyebrows an' eye-lashes an' hawf o' t' hair hed been swinge't off me heed. Efter fastenin' t' dooars togidder, t' seame set com back an' set fire till a lot o' powder just as I went oot till them, an' luik what a seet they've meade me. But I've fund oot whea they are, an' bleame me!' he added, striking the table again, 'I'll hev them hanged if I hev to dee t' job mesel'. Hooiver, Misther Sumerville, I didn't cum here to talk till ye aboot mesel'. I com wid a messige for this gentleman here.'"

And he pointed to Robert Fenwood.

# CHAPTER IV.

—o—

" Judge we by nature ?—habit may efface,
  Interest o'ercome, or policy take place ;
  By actions ?—these uncertainty divides ;
  By passions ?—these dissimulation hides ;
  Opinions ?—these still take a wider range.
  Find, if you can, in what you cannot change,
  Manners with fortunes, humours turn with climes,
  Tenets with books, and principles with times."—*Pope.*

"A MESSAGE for me !" said Fenwood, in amazement. " Who is it from ?"

" That I can't tell yé," answered the man. " Just as I was cumin' on t' road, a young chap says till me, ' Div ye know Misther Fenwood ?' ' Be seet,' says I, ' I div.' ' Div you know wor he is ?' says t' chap. ' No,' says I, ' I divn't, widoot he's at heame.' ' Oh,' says t' young fellow, ' he isn't theear.' ' Weel than,' says I, ' he's mebbe at Misther Sumerville's.' ' Misther Sumerville !' says t' chap, ' whea's he ?' ' Wey, thoo mun be a agymoramus nut to know Misther Sumerville ! Wey barne——' "

" But, man," interrupted Fenwood, impatiently, " will you be kind enough to come to the point, and tell me what your message is ?"

" Isn't I tellin' yé ?" retorted Jenkins, indignantly. " ' A agymoramus,' says I, ' nut to know—out to know—' Loavins bless us aw weel ! what was it 'at he dudn't know ? Them lads, last neet, hes completely knock't senses out o' me !"

Robert Fenwood made a gesture of impatience.

"Divn't toss the' arms aboot like a clot-heid, min!" said Jenkins, angrily. "I was gitten on reet anuef till thoo pot the' oar in. Oh, I hev it noo! 'If he's at Misther Sumerville's,' says t' young chap, 'gang theear and tell him that he's to git heame as fast as he can, for t' old woman 'at keeps hoose for him 's tyan a fit.'"

"Good heavens!" said Fenwood, starting from his seat; "and here have you been standing chattering like a magpie for a quarter of an hour, and never told me this till now!"

"That's t' thenks a fellow gits for deein' a gud turn," said Jenkins, turning with a meek and resigned air to the farmer. "But I luik't for nowt better. T' cat and t' kitlins com out o' t' smoothin' iron: Jinkins o' Cleator Moor."

Without waiting to ask for an explanation as to what Mr. Jenkins meant by his concluding remarks, the colliery manager hurriedly seized his hat, and prepared to depart.

"You will excuse me, Mr. and Mrs. Somerville, I am sure," he said: "and you, Mary, also. My housekeeper may be dying, and I don't know that there is any one with her."

"Does te' nut?" said Jenkins. "Ay, than, I know that there is. T' young chap said to me, 'I went till t' hoose to luik for Misther Fenwood,' says he, 'an' t' oald woman answer't t' dooar. I ax'd if he was in, an' she was just gahn to say summat, when she tummel't doon aw ov a heap. I got a woman to gang an' bide wid her; an' I want somebody to gang an' tell her maister.' An' I've cum't an' tell't the', and a bonny star thoo is to tell owt tull!"

"Hod the' noise, Jimmy," said the farmer, angrily, "an' doon't carry on like that here. Thoo's gone clean crack't awtogidder."

"Ye're aboot reet," muttered Jenkins, "or else I wad niver ha' cum't on sec a fuil's errand as this. Dang me! if my pooar auld mudder, that's liggin' in her grave, had iver ha' thowt that I wad ha' acted sa daft as this, she wad ha' bray't me heid till it was as soft as a boil'd taytee!" And turning on his heel in intense disgust and indignation, Mr. Jenkins walked out of the room.

"I can't varra weel leave t' hoose," said Mrs. Somerville to Fenwood, "or else I wad gang and see if I cud dee t' oald woman any gud. But Mary'll tak a slip ower wid yé, and give any help she can."

The young woman frowned on hearing the words of her mother; but as Robert Fenwood turned eagerly and anxiously towards her, her countenance cleared up, and she expressed her readiness to accompany him. They left the farm together, and pursued their way almost in silence, until they reached the solitary house where Fenwood lived.

The old housekeeper was in bed. She had been struck down by a fit of paralysis which had deprived her of speech, and her hard features were drawn up and distorted by the attack. A woman, whose assistance had been obtained by the young man who had visited the dwelling in search of the colliery manager, sat by the side of the sufferer. When Fenwood and Mary entered the room where she was lying, the housekeeper turned a look upon them so sad and ghastly, that the tears gushed into Mary Somerville's eyes. The colliery manager went up to the bedside, and said—

" What is the matter, Ann ? What is it that ails you ?"

The sufferer made an effort to answer, but in vain.

" She can't talk," said the woman who was sitting beside her, " seay it's neay use axin' her any questins. She's hed a stroke."

Fenwood looked first at one of the women and then at the other. He was visibly moved—more so than Mary Somerville had ever seen him, and his face was almost as white as a sheet.

" Has anybody gone for a doctor ?" he inquired.

" Ay," said the woman ; " t' young chap that com to late ye 's dun that. Theear's neeay doctor narder than Whitehebben, and seay he's gone theear."

" Has he been long gone ?" asked Fenwood.

" A gud bit," was the reply. " He borrowed a horse to tak him. He'll be back suin, I sud say."

Robert Fenwood and Mary sat down in the room, and the most profound silence was maintained by all present. The woman who had been called in was evidently not disposed to talk ; the colliery manager was in no mood for conversation ; and Mary was so painfully affected by the the sight of the housekeeper hovering between life and death, that she had no inclination to utter a word.

The silence became oppressive at last, and all present felt it to be a relief when the sound of a horse's hoofs was heard approaching the house. Shortly afterwards the sound ceased, and a knock was heard at the door.

" He's here at last," muttered the woman, as she rose from her seat and hastened downstairs. In a short time

she returned, followed by a slender, dark-featured young
man, in whom Fenwood recognised an overman employed
at the colliery of which he had the management.

"Is that you, Jones?" said Fenwood.

"Yes," replied the young man, "it is. I saw the doctor, and he'll be here directly. He was making ready to
set off when I left. Dear me, dear me, what a sad job!"

Mr. Jones took his hat off, wiped the perspiration from
his forehead with his pocket handkerchief, and then shaking his head with a melancholy air, said, by way of
improving the occasion—

"Ah! in the midst of death we are in life. But," he
added, suddenly striking out into a new field, "I've left
the horse standing at the door, and perhaps it may run
away. It doesn't belong to me; I borrowed it from
Wilfrid Mumberson, so I'll take it back to him. I wanted
to speak to you about some business, Mr. Fenwood, but it
will keep till to-morrow."

He bade them good night, and left the house. About
half-an-hour after his departure the doctor arrived. He
was a little, spare, elderly man, clerical in appearance,
with a shrewd penetrating look. Stepping briskly to the
bed on which the paralysed woman lay, he placed his
finger upon her wrist, and then scanned her features
attentively. Those present saw that as he did so, his own
face assumed a very grave look.

"Is she seriously ill, doctor?" said Fenwood, breaking
the painful silence.

"Yes," was the reply, "she is. I concluded from what
the young man who came for me told me, that it was an
attack of paralysis, and I have brought some medicine

with me which must be given to her. Beyond that, nothing can be done for her at present. If she should change for the worse, come for me as quickly as possible. I don't know that I shall be able to do any good; but still, if you will let me know, I shall be glad to come and do what I can. Good night."

After giving some instructions as to the treatment of the patient the doctor left, and in a short time the persons in the room heard him galloping away.

" You have no objection to stay with her, Mrs. ——— I don't know your name," said Fenwood, addressing the woman.

" Sally Jeffreys is my name," was the reply.

" You have no objection to stay with her, Mrs. Jeffreys," said Fenwood, indicating the housekeeper, " and attend to her, provided I pay you well for your services ? "

" Nut a bit," answered Mrs. Jeffreys; " but ye'll hev to gang on till our hoose, about fifty yards on t' road at t' left hand side, and tell them I can't git heame. Pay !" she continued; I'se thinkin' nowt aboot that. We aw stand in need o' sumbody to luik efter us when we're badly, and I wad be a hardened Turk to gang and leave a pooar old creetur liggin' i' this state, and nut yable to git a drink o' watter for hersel'."

" Then Mary," said Fenwood, turning to his sweetheart, " it will be unnecessary for you to stay any longer; so, if you like I will see you home. Mrs. Jeffreys can manage well enough till my return."

" If I could be of any service," said Mary, " I should be glad to return in the morning."

" Thank you," said Fenwood, " for the offer; and if you can spare the time, I shall be happy to see you."

They went away together, and after Fenwood had seen Mary safely into her father's house, he returned to his own.

The following morning, after breakfast, Mary Somerville walked over to the residence of the colliery manager. She found him walking about in a room down stairs, evidently in a very disturbed and uneasy state. He greeted Mary, however, very kindly, and asked her to walk upstairs and see the old housekeeper.

The young woman complied with the request. On entering the room, Mary saw at once that a change for the worse had taken place in the condition of the sufferer. Her cheeks had fallen in, her eyes were turned to the ceiling with a fixed and stony glare; and plainly gathering around her was the shadow of a long eternal night.

" She seems worse than she was yesterday," whispered Mary to Fenwood.

" I think so," replied he, in a low voice. " What do you think, Mrs. Jeffreys," he added, speaking to the woman, who still sat by the side of the bed, " about my going to Whitehaven, and asking the doctor to come and see Ann?"

" I think ye'd better," said the woman, quietly.

" Mary will remain with you till I come back."

" She can owther gang or stay, just as she likes," said Mrs Jeffreys, coldly.

" I suppose you have no objection to stay here till my return?" said Fenwood, turning to the young woman.

" None in the world," she replied.

He at once set out upon his errand, and the two women were left alone with the housekeeper. Mary felt rather embarrassed, for Mrs. Jeffreys was in a surly mood—at least her companion thought so—and returned very curt replies to any questions that were addressed to her. At last the young woman rose from her seat.

" I will go down stairs a short time, Mrs. Jeffreys," she said; " but I am not going to leave the house. If you want me you can call me."

The woman gave a grunt by way of answer, and Mary went down stairs. The house was not a large one, but it was a pleasant place enough, and very comfortably furnished. When she reached the ground floor, Mary saw two doors, one on the right and the other on the left hand. The one on the left hand opened into the room where she had seen Fenwood on her arrival that morning. Acting upon a sudden impulse, she turned the handle of the door upon her right, and entered the apartment into which it led.

The furniture of the room was plain but substantial, and on a table in its centre lay pens, ink, and a quantity of paper. Mary advanced to the window, which opened out upon the Moor, and looked long and earnestly at the wild and dreary scene before her. And as she looked, a flood of recollections came rushing through her mind. She thought of the past, of her slighted lover, of her own position, of the strange man in whose house she was, of the dying woman above, of the dark and impenetrable future before her ; and the tears of remorse and sorrow sprang unbidden to her eyes.

" What will be the end of it ?" she murmured, " God only knows ; for I cannot tell."

She turned from the window and approached the table. Amongst the papers lying upon it were several sheets containing writing, folded carefully within each other. She felt conscious that she was doing wrong; but she could not resist the temptation to look at the writing. It was that of Fenwood. She read about half-way down the first page, and then with a sudden gasp placed one hand upon her heart, and grasped the table with the other to prevent herself from falling, whilst her face went as white as that of a corpse. Recovering her composure by a strong and resolute effort, Mary Somerville sat down at the table, and read the terrible revelation which follows :—

   *   *   *   *   *
   *   *   *   *   *

" I don't know whether I should call this a confession or not. Perhaps that is the right name for it ; perhaps it is not. I don't know what it is that forces me—*forces,* that is the word—to commit to paper what I certainly ought to keep in my own breast. For who knows, notwithstanding my solitary mode of life—secluded as I keep myself—some prying eyes may glance over this paper, and some inquisitive being may learn that the soul of the writer is stained with the crime of—MURDER !

" It cost me a great effort to write that last word. I would much rather, if I could help it, not write anything concerning that awful deed, the recollection of which haunts my sleeping and waking hours ; but I feel compelled, against my will, to proceed. I have heard of men who felt tempted to curse their Creator and scream out the most horrible blasphemies. I have heard of men who felt tempted to commit murder. Some of them yielded to the temptation which beset them; others, sooner than yield, took away their own lives. There is something standing beside me now which controls all my movements. An unseen hand is guiding my pen, and a voice is whispering in my ear—'Walter Daneson, write!' And I must obey the command. I cannot help myself.

"Let me think for a moment before I proceed any further.

"I was born at Blaydon, near Newcastle. My father, Henry Daneson, was a thriving tradesman there. He had two sons—myself and my brother Wilfrid, younger than I. Wilfrid was from childhood weak and sickly, and my father and mother almost idolised him. About myself they seemed to care very little—at least I thought so. I was strong and hardy, and well able to take care of myself. They knew that, and reserved all their tenderness for the sickly, puling lad. Their treatment of us was so different that I believe it was the cause which led me to hate my brother.

"I recollect when that hatred came upon me very well. Wilfrid had been out walking, and had returned home weary and worn out. At that time he was fourteen, and I seventeen, years of age. As he sat with his head upon his hand, breathing hard, I looked at him closely. Why, said I, should he be so much more thought of than I am? Why do my parents think so little of me and such a great deal of him? What right has he to all their affection? And then the thought flashed through my mind as quick as lightning—It would be better if he was dead!

"If a pit had suddenly and unexpectedly opened at my feet, I could scarcely have started back in greater terror

than I did from that thought when it first came across me.
But it clung to me; I tried to shake it off, but I tried in
vain. It haunted me constantly; it was always upper-
most in mind; and it tormented me to that extent that I
was nearly driven mad. If I had only gone mad outright,
it would have been a blessing.

"I was employed then as assistant bookkeeper at a
colliery not far from Blaydon. My brother followed no
profession—indeed, he was not strong enough to follow
any. The most of his time was spent at home, for he was
so feeble that he could not stir out much. He was, I
believe, as gentle and as good a lad as ever lived; and
although I invariably treated him harshly, no unkind
word to me ever passed his lips. My father and mother
saw the dislike with which I regarded him, and many a
time was I censured by them for my want of brotherly
affection. Their reproaches only added fuel to the evil
fire which was consuming me, and in my blind hatred I
blamed my brother for the consequences of my own conduct.

"I come now to speak of the crime which blasted my
peace for ever, and made my life a hell. I had reached
the age of twenty-one years; Wilfrid was eighteen. He
was suffering from consumption, the seeds of which had
been in his system from boyhood, and at last the dreadful
disease manifested itself in its full force. He moved about
as long as he could, but eventually his strength failed completely, and he was confined to his bed. My father and
mother were almost heart-broken at the prospect of losing
their darling son; and I—well, I felt a gloomy satisfaction in watching him sink gradually, day by day, in notic-

ing the hectic flush upon the cheek, the difficult breathing, and the weary, sad look in the patient face. Poor fellow! He never murmured. He was at an age when life appears the fairest, when the world and its beauties and pleasures have the most attraction for the heart and mind, when the present is like a glorious day in summer, and the future bright with hope; and it was at such an age that he was called upon to exchange this world for another, life for death, time for eternity. But he never repined; he was completely resigned to his fate; and the only words he used when alluding to it were those spoken by Jesus in the garden of Gethsemane—'Father, not my will, but thine be done.'

# CHAPTER V.

—o—

"Nothing but lifeless flesh and bone,
   That could not do me ill;
And yet I feared him all the more,
   For lying there so still.
There was a manhood in his look,
   That murder could not kill."—*Hood.*

"I RECOLLECT the time very well. I have a good reason for doing so. It was a mild evening in September. I had just returned home from work, and found my mother sitting alone by the fire, weeping. I knew the cause of her sorrow, and it was therefore unnecessary to question her about it. My father came into the room where my mother and I were, looking very sorrowful, and sat down without speaking. For some time not a word was said by any of us. At last my mother broke the silence.

"'How is Wilfrid now?'

"'As bad as he well can be,' replied my father. 'The doctor doesn't expect him to live through the night.'

"My mother wept more bitterly than ever; and my father tried hard for a time to keep the tears back, but his efforts to do so were useless, and at length he covered his face with his hands, and cried bitterly. I sat looking at both of them, moody and silent.

"'Walter,' said my father, when the violence of his grief had rather abated, 'go and sit with Wilfrid. He is quite alone, and very ill. If he changes for the worse, let us know.'

" Without speaking, I rose from my seat and proceeded to the room where my brother lay. When I entered it he was lying with his eyes closed, apparently asleep. He was worn almost to a skeleton ; his hands, which rested upon the coverlet of the bed, were almost transparent ; and on the thin white face death had plainly set its seal.

" I advanced to the bedside, and pronounced his name.

" He opened his eyes and smiled.

" ' Is that you, Walter ? ' he said, in a voice so low that it was little more than a whisper. ' I am glad to see you. Sit down.'

" I did so, and looked at him closely.

" ' Ah, Walter,' he continued, ' I am going to leave you. The doctor tells me that I cannot live much longer. I am sorry that we have not been better friends—very sorry that you have kept away from me, and treated me so coldly, for I have always loved you, and I love you now very dearly. God only knows the pain which our estrangement has caused me.'

" I made him no answer. Like a flash the thought passed through my mind—' You are alone with him ; he is helpless ; he cannot even call for assistance ; kill him.' It was a horrible thought, and it made the flesh creep on my bones, but I could not get rid of it. My brother was sinking fast ; his days, ay, his hours were numbered. Why should I cut short that blameless life ; why should I murder one who loved me dearly ; why should I stain my hands with blood, and that blood the blood of my trusting brother ? These thoughts also passed through my mind ; but the devil at my side was not to be satisfied with such an answer, and whispered in my ear more fiercely than ever—' You and he are alone ; kill him.'

" Instead of falling upon my knees, and praying earnestly to God to remove the temptation far from me, I yielded to it. Instead of rushing from the room and leaving the feeble youth to breathe his last in peace, I remained with him.

" I rose from my seat and stooped over him. The evil thought which possessed me must have shown itself in my face, for I noticed his assume a look of alarm, and he said, hastily—

" ' Walter, what is the matter with you ? What a strange look you have ! '

" ' Have I ? ' said I, with a forced laugh ; and I turned and glanced round the room.

" In one corner there stood a table, on which were a wash-hand basin, a jug containing water, and a towel. There was little fear of my father or mother disturbing us ; but I saw the necessity of doing what I had to do quickly. I went to the table, took the towel, dipped it in the water, and then wrung it. When this was done I folded it carefully, and hurried to the bedside.

" ' Walter ! ' said my brother, with terror in his face ; ' what are you going to do ? My God ! ' he added, trying to spring out of bed ; 'what do you mean by this conduct?'

" I never spoke, but taking the wet folded towel in both hands, pressed it firmly over his mouth and nostrils. He struggled as well as he could, but he was too far spent to struggle much. A little while after he had ceased to move I removed the towel.

E

" My brother was dead.

" I stood looking at him. His face was as composed as
if he were asleep, and there was a smile upon it. No
language that was ever written or spoken could describe
my feelings as I gazed at the dead youth. I would have
given worlds freely if they would only have brought him
back to life ; I would have suffered any torture, no matter
how great, if I could only have heard that kind voice once
more. Henceforth I was doomed to walk the earth with
the brand of Cain upon my brow ; and the devil who had
prompted me to commit the fearful crime seemed now to
mock my misery.

" My remorse for the murder of my brother quickly
gave place to fear of the consequences to myself if the
crime should be found out. My mode of action, however,
was quickly decided upon. I concealed the towel beneath
my waistcoat, and wiped the face of the corpse quite dry
with my pocket handkerchief. I gave one last look at
that face so placid, with the smile resting upon the dead
features, and then I rushed wildly from the room.

" My parents were sitting down stairs as I had left
them ; but when I entered my mother raised her head
quickly. She must have seen by my look that something
was wrong, for she cried out—

" ' Is there anything amiss, Walter ? Is Wilfrid
worse ? '

" ' I think so,' said I, hoarsely. ' A change came over
him while I was with him.'

" She waited to hear no more, but hurried upstairs,
followed by my father, to where my murdered brother lay.
Shortly afterwards a scream, which pierced my brain like

an arrow, rang through the house, and I buried my face in my hands, and groaned aloud in agony of heart. I heard footsteps moving about hurriedly overhead, and my father's voice calling me.

" I would have given my right arm to have avoided entering that room again. I dreaded the sight of that dead boy, slain by my hand. But there was no alternative. So, summoning to my aid a bastard courage, I went upstairs.

" My mother was lying senseless upon the bed beside her darling son. My father was pacing the apartment like a distracted man.

" ' Oh, Walter !' he exclaimed on seeing me. 'Wilfrid is dead !'

" I started back in pretended amazement.

" ' Walter,' he continued, 'how is this ? Was your brother alive when you left him ?'

" ' I can scarcely tell,' was my reply : 'but I think so. A change came over him while I sat beside him, and when I saw it I hurried down to you.'

" ' He has gone very suddenly at last,' said my father ; and then he added, with a passionate burst of sorrow, ' Oh, Wilfrid, my son, my son, would to God I had died for thee !'

" Presently he turned upon me, with a quickness which startled me.

" ' How was it,' he asked sternly, 'that you did not call your mother and myself when you saw your brother getting worse ?'

" ' I tell you that as soon as I saw him getting worse I came down and told you,' was my reply.

"In a short time my mother recovered her senses; but the violence of her grief, and that of my father, was terrible. And what were my feelings? I was standing in the room where, not half-an-hour before, I had coolly and deliberately extinguished the feeble spark of life in one who had never injured mortal, and who would have made any sacrifice to gain my affection. If it had not been for my fear of that unknown eternity—the awful realities of which have never been disclosed—I would then and there have put an end to my own wretched and worse than worthless existence.

"I was sent out for the doctor. The medical man, when I told him that my brother was dead, looked at me in surprise.

"'It's very strange,' he said. 'I knew that he had not long to live, but I never expected he would have died so soon. Why have you come for me? I can be of no service now.'

"'My father wishes to see you,' was my answer.

"The doctor put on his hat, and walked back with me to the house. My parents were still in the room with the corpse. When the medical man entered, he did not speak a word to either of them, but went forward and looked long and earnestly at my dead brother.

"It is a most remarkable thing,' he said at last, turning to my father. 'Who was with him when he died?"

"'No one,' answered my father.

"'No one!' repeated the doctor, in astonishment.

"'No,' said my father. 'His brother here came up to sit with him awhile, and during the time he was in the room the poor lad became worse. Walter came down to tell us about him, and we at once hurried up here, but only to find him dead.'

"The medical man fastened a look upon me that made my heart die away within me. But I felt the necessity of preserving my composure, and I returned the gaze with one as calm and steady as I could command.

"'How long were you with him before this change took place?' the doctor asked.

"'Not very long,' I replied. 'Indeed he seemed as if he was dying when I entered the room.'

"'Did you call any one?'

"'As soon as I saw that he was sinking so fast, I went down stairs and told my father and mother.'

"'Was he alive then?'

"'I cannot be certain, but I think he was.'

"The medical man stood silent, and in deep thought, for some time.

"'It is unaccountable,' he said at length, looking up, 'that he should have passed away in this manner. Of course he never had the slightest chance of getting better; but that he should have died almost in a moment, and unseen, does certainly astonish me.'

"The doctor shortly afterwards took his departure, and I noticed, as he left, that his face wore a puzzled and dissatisfied look. Clearly he was quite at a loss to account for the strange and startingly sudden death of Wilfrid; but it appeared equally clear he had no suspicion that that death was caused by violence. Indeed, how could he— how could any one—have any such suspicion? No human eye had witnessed that awful scene, one of the actors in which was a dastardly coward, blinded by a bitter and unnatural hatred, and animated by the spirit of the devil; and the other a poor lad, struggling feebly but hopelessly against the attempt to crush out his life.

"I went to bed that night, and tried to sleep. I might as well have tried to remove a mountain with my hand, or turn back the tide with a word. In a room not far from me lay the corpse, and my father and mother were watching it. They asked me to sit with them, but I pleaded illness as a reason for declining, and the plea was accepted. If it would have saved me from the gallows I could not have complied with their request. The sight of that white face, those fixed features, coupled with the knowledge of my fearful crime, would have driven me mad. As it was, in the darkness of my own room I saw my brother just as when, evidently divining my horrid purpose, he attempted, with a look of alarm, to spring out of bed. I tried to shut the sight out by closing my eyes. I tossed and turned, and moaned in misery; I covered my face with my hands; I left my bed in terror, and groping my way to a chair, sat down upon it; but do what I would, go where I would, the face of my dead brother looked steadily into mine.

"From that night up to the present hour I have never lost sight of that face. I see it now as plainly as I saw it then. And if perpetual wretchedness, if sleepless nights and weary days, if for long years never to have known peace for a moment, if to drag out existence with a constant fear that my crime will in some unexpected way, and by some unexpected means, be made known to the world, if the dread of a shameful death, be any punishment, most assuredly I have been, and am still punished.

" My brother was buried, and I attended the funeral. It was a large funeral, for he was well known and generally beloved. As I stood by the side of the grave, looking at the people assembled, I could not help thinking what their feelings would be, and how they would regard me, if they only knew the truth.

" My father and mother were a long time before they got over the loss of their favourite. At last time kindly healed the wounds caused by that loss, and they began to manifest more affection for myself than they had ever done before. But every kind word which they uttered was simply a dagger planted in my breast. I could find no rest anywhere. That death struggle—that awful face —my God! how they haunted me—how they haunt me still! From bookkeeper I was promoted to be assistant manager of the colliery where I was employed. I allied myself to a religious Dissenting body, and became one of its most active members ; but those who listened at our meetings to my fierce condemnation of sin and crime little suspected what a heavy weight of guilt rested on my own soul. I found, however, that my religious zeal—or rather my pretended religious zeal—raised me more than almost anything else could have done in the estimation of the people by whom I was surrounded—and to my other sins I added that of hypocrisy. Notwithstanding the estimation in which I was held generally, Blaydon became at last absolutely insupportable to me, and I longed to get away from it, hoping that a change of place would alleviate my woe. The post of manager of a colliery in this wild, solitary district fell vacant, and I applied for it. Through the influence of friends and a good character I

obtained the appointment ; and here I am, known not as
Walter Daneson, but as Robert Fenwood, more miserable
than ever, striving ever and always to forget that awful
look in the face of my brother ere he was killed, but striving in vain."

*　　　*　　　*　　　*　　　*
*　　　*　　　*　　　*　　　*

Here the manuscript ended ; but for some time after she
had finished it, the terrified reader sat with her eyes fixed
upon the record of guilt as if she had been turned into
stone.    Mingled with the sickening and horror which the
confession of crime had created within her, was a feeling
of thankfulness that her eyes had been opened to the true
character of the vile ruffian whose hands were stained
with blood.    He had not, as yet, plainly avowed his love,
or asked her to become his wife, and she was determined,
if it were possible, that he should never have the chance
of doing so.    From that day henceforth she would avoid
him as she would a serpent.

Once she thought seriously of taking possession of the
manuscript, leaving the house with it, and placing it in
the hands of the authorities, so that Walter Daneson, *alias*
Robert Fenwood, might be brought to justice.    But, after
a little consideration, she decided against the adoption of
this course.    She felt that she had not acted honourably
in entering a private room and reading that which was
never intended for her eyes.    And even if, through her
instrumentality, the murderer should be made to expiate
the fearful crime which he had committed upon the scaf-
fold, what good would she accomplish by his death ?    It

would be the better plan, she reasoned, to keep the knowledge which she had obtained to herself, and never to use it, unless compelled to do so by Fenwood himself.

She sprang from her seat in dismay, as the thought flashed through her mind that the colliery manager might return suddenly and find her in that room. Placing the manuscript exactly in the same position as that in which she had found it, the young woman hurried from the apartment with as much haste as if a thunderbolt had crashed into it through the ceiling.

Mary Somerville was not usually very nervous, but her knees trembled beneath her, and she felt sick at heart, as she went up to the room where the housekeeper lay ill. On entering it, the young woman found Mrs. Jeffreys sitting in the position in which she had left her, and the patient lying so quiet and motionless, that it seemed as if she were either dead or asleep.

"Ye've been oot a gay bit," said Mrs. Jeffreys to Mary, without turning her head.

"Yes," was the reply, delivered in a low voice. "Have you wanted me?"

"No."

"Is there any alteration in her?" said Mary, indicating the patient.

"Yis, for t' warse," was the curt reply.

"Is she not likely to recover?"

"Nowt o' t' mak."

"Poor thing!" said Mary, and her eyes filled with tears as she looked at the distorted face.

"Ay," muttered the watcher, 'yé may weel say that. Deeth taks sum when they're yung, and udders when they're oald ; but we aw hev to gang t'ya road sum time, an' its a hard road to travel, whether we're oald or yung.''

The tears which had gathered in the eyes of Mary Somerville now began to flow freely, and at last, completely overcome by the sight of the sufferer before her, and the horror inspired by the fearful story she had read during her absence from the room, the young woman gave way to a burst of grief, so violent and bitter, that even the stolid Mrs. Jeffreys was alarmed by it.

"Wey, whativer's t' matter wid yé ?" said that good lady, turning round, and looking at her attentively.

" Oh, Mrs. Jeffreys,'' exclaimed Mary, wringing her hands, and sobbing like a child, '' I cannot remain here, I want to go home !''

" Varra weel, me lass,'' returned Mrs. Jeffreys, '' away yé gang ; but what ails yé ?'''

"I can scarcely tell,'' replied the young woman, ''My head aches ; I feel such a dreadful sinking at the heart ; and—God help me !—I think I am going distracted.''

" Well, then, ye'd better gang heam,'' said Mrs. Jeffreys, '' because if ye're t' way that yé say yé ur, ye're nut reet But hedn't yé better stop till Misther Fenwood cums ? He can't be seay varra lang noo.''

With a cry which rang through the room, Mary Somerville rose from her seat, and stretched out her hands as if to ward off something evil.

The watcher by the sick bed looked at her in amazement ; but presently her attention was called in another direction. The sick woman gave a low moan, and Mrs. Jeffreys rose and bent over her. Then she raised her finger, and Mary, making a strong effort to be calm, went forward and stood beside her.

" She's gahn fast," said the watcher, in a low voice.

The dying woman made an effort to move, and a low sigh came from her lips. This was followed by a slight quiver of the eyelids, and that peculiar sound in the throat which is the sure precursor of death. At last the motion and the sound ceased, and an awful change, which death alone can produce, passed over the face.

" She's gone," said Mrs. Jeffreys, after a few moments' pause; " an' here," she added, as footsteps were heard ascending the stairs, " is Misther Fenwood an' t' doctor, I'll be bund."

Her conjecture was right. When Robert Fenwood and the medical man entered, Mary Somerville shrank in dread and aversion from the former as he passed her and hurried to the bedside.

"How is she?" said he to Mrs. Jeffreys.

By way of answer, the woman turned down the coverlet which concealed the features with one hand, and pointed with the forefinger of the other at the face.

" Good heavens!" cried Fenwood, starting back, "is she dead?" Then he added, looking eagerly round the room, " Where is Miss Somerville?"

Mary Somerville was not to be seen. She had left the house.

# CHAPTER VI.

—o—

" Of all the numerous ills that hurt our peace,
That press the soul, or wring the mind with anguish,
Beyond comparison, the worst are those
That to our folly or our guilt we owe.
In every other circumstance, the mind
Has this to say—' It was no deed of mine.'
But when to all the evil of misfortune
This sting is added—' Blame thy foolish self,'—
O burning hell! in all thy store of torments,
There's not a keener lash."—*Blair*.

MARY SOMERVILLE breathed more freely when she got into the open air, and hurried along the road as rapidly as she could towards her own home. How she reached it she scarcely knew, but upon her arrival at the farm the young woman at once proceeded to her own room, where she could think alone.

The confession of crime which she had read at the house of Robert Fenwood had done more to open her eyes to the folly and sin of her frivolous conduct than anything else could have done. That it should have produced such an effect is scarcely to be wondered at. It was absolutely appalling to reflect that she had been coquetting with a man—if man he could be called—who from a sheer love of murder had slain his own brother. In addition to this, she felt that the terrible secret which she had learnt would press heavily upon her own mind, if it did not render her life one perpetual round of torture.

Her thoughts wandered to James Blaylock. How bitterly she began to regret her harsh and cruel treatment of one of the bravest and noblest hearts that ever beat in the breast of man; and how keenly did she now feel the estrangement which her own conduct had caused !

"My sin has found me," she murmured, as she pressed her hands upon her face to keep back the bitter tears which gathered in her eyes. "Poor James! Will he ever come back to me?"

After the lapse of a considerable time, she became a little calmer, and went from her own room to the kitchen below, where the family were assembled at dinner.

"What, Mary," said her father, "is that thee? Hoo's Misther Fenwood's hoosekeeper gitten' on?"

Mary shuddered at the mention of the name; but she replied, with as much composure as she could command—

"The housekeeper is dead."

"Deed!" exclaimed her mother. "Loavins bless us aw weel, lass! what's t' matter thoo didn't tell us that till noo?"

"Mother," said Mary, "I did not feel well when I came in, and I was compelled to go to my own room."

"An' t' pooar oald body's gone!" said the farmer. "Well, well, it can't be help't; the Lord gev, and the Lord hes a reet to tak when he thinks fit. Was te' theear when she deed?"

"Yes."

"Hoo is Misther Fenwood hissel'?" inquired the farmer.

Mary's face went very pale, and she breathed hard, as if she had been running. It was some time before she could reply, but at last she said, in a low voice—

"I don't know."

"Nut know! Hoo's that!" exclaimed her father, in surprise.

The young woman rose from the table with a gesture expressive of loathing and horror.

"Father, father," she said, "I implore you, if you have any love for me, not to mention the name of Fenwood in in my hearing!" And then turning away, she walked swiftly out of the room.

" T' deeth o' that oald body," said her father, " hes sent her daft. But what is I nut to mention Misther Fenwood's neame for ? What hes he dun ? Theear's a wol i' t' ballad, that's plain annuf. She beats aw t' lasses 'at iver I saw i' my life. She gev yung Jimmy Blaylock t' seck, and hoc many chaps she's seck'd awtogidder it's unpossable to tell. Noo than Misther Fenwood's got in her black buiks. I isn't to menshun his neame. I'll be hanged if she won't carry on till she'll nut be yable to git a husband at aw just noo, nowder for luive nor munney."

" She's nobbet yung yit," pleaded Mrs. Somerville; " she'll git mair sense just noo. Mebbe Misther Fenwood's dun summat to affrunt her."

" Affrunt her !" repeated the farmer, with a start, whilst a flush overspread his bronzed and honest face. " If I thowt seay——But no," he added, " it isn't likely. He's yan o' oor local preachers, an' aboot t' best we hev—far better than many a travellin' preacher—he's a real decent, upreet fellow, if iver theear was yan ; and I'se confident 'at he waddent say a wrang wurd nor dui a wrang thing tull mortal."

The farmer was evidently not satisfied, however, for when he rose from his seat, he said—

" Wor is Mary gone ?"

" I think she's off tull her oan room agean," said Mrs. Somerville. " What for ?"

" I mun see her," muttered the farmer.

He ascended the stairs, and quietly entered his daughter's apartment. The young woman was lying upon the bed, with her face resting upon the pillow, and sobbing as if her heart would break.

" Mary !" said her father.

She started up with a scream, and looked wildly around the room. At last she cried out—

" Oh, father, is it you ?"

" It is," was the reply, " What ails the', me lass ?"

She passed her hands across her brow, and sighing deeply, said, in a low, sad voice—

" I feel very ill, father."

" Mary," said the farmer, " when thoo was down t' stairs, thoo said I wasn't to menshun Misther Fenwood's neame tull the'. Noo, I isn't gahn to say much aboot him ; but I want to ax the' a question or two. Hes thee and him fell oot ?"

" No," said Mary, with a shudder, " we have not."

" Hes he dun or said owt amiss till the' ?"

" No."

" Than what's t' matter, anyway ?"

" Do not ask me, father, oh, do not ask me !" replied the young woman, distractedly. He has neither done nor said anything wrong to me ; but if you have any love for me, and I know you have, never speak his name in my hearing."

" Well," muttered the farmer, " I can mak nowder heid nor tail o' this. What in t' neame o' fortin's t' reason o' aw this bodder?"

" Father," said the young woman, falling on her knees before him, " listen to me for a moment. You have often charged me with being thoughtless, and I feel that the charge is true. But if my thoughtlessness and giddiness have ever caused you a moment's pain, if my conduct has at any time brought sorrow to your heart, forgive me, and believe me when I say, that I am truly sorry for what I have done."

" Tut, tut, lass," said her father, his lips quivering with emotion, " thoo munnet gang on like this. I was yance yung mesel'. I knew it wad aw cum reet annuf at last, an' that thoo wad niver dui owt to sham owder thesel' or me. I wad far rayder ha' seen the' stiddier; but yung lasses will be yung lasses, an' yan can't put oald heids on yung showlders. Theear's nowt to fret aboot. Lig doon agean, an' try to git a bit o' sleep; it 'll dui the' gud."

The young woman threw herself upon the bed, and her father left her.

" Theear's neay chance," he muttered to himself, as he walked down the stairs, " of Misther Fenwood an' her makin' a pair. I'se fairly baffled. She says he's nowder dun nor said owt amiss till her, an' yit his neame isn't to be menshun'd agean. Theear's a screw lowse sumway, but wor it is I can't tell."

He thought about the interview between himself and his daughter many times that day.

Mary Somerville remained in her own apartment till the evening came. She could think of nothing but the dreadful narrative which she had read in the morning. Her excited fancy pictured the chamber in which lay the dying lad, and she saw the murderer bending over him and choking out his life. That look upon the face, which the assassin declared haunted his sleeping and waking hours —she beheld it as distinctly as if the victim had stood before her, and she wished from the bottom of her heart that she had never seen or known Robert Fenwood.

She came down stairs after sunset, and was told that Fenwood had visited the house and expressed a desire to see her. But he had been informed that she was ill, and had left without pressing his request.

Three days afterwards the old housekeeper was buried. Mr. and Mrs. Somerville attended the funeral, but Mary felt such a dread of meeting Fenwood again that she remained at home. She heard, however, that a woman from Whitehaven had taken the housekeeper's place.

The day after the funeral the colliery manager paid another visit to the residence of the farmer. From the window of the room in which she was sitting Mary saw him approaching, and the colour fled from her cheeks. Without speaking a word, she left the place and hurried to her own chamber, where she remained until she saw him leave, about an hour afterwards. Then she again joined her father and mother.

" Thoo said I was nut to menshun Misther Fenwood's neame till the' agean, Mary," said the farmer, evidently annoyed; " but I can't help deein' it. He's been here, an'

E

he's gone away quite vex't. What hes he dun anyway, I ax the' agean, that thoo wont luik at him ?"

"Oh, father," replied the young woman, " ask me no questions."

" But I'se forced to ax the' questins," said the farmer. " I can't affrunt folk widoot tellin' them what it's for. When he cums agean and axes efter the', is I to tell him that thoo won't see him at aw ?"

The face of Mary became very white, and she stood silent for a short time. At last she said, in a low voice—

" You can tell him what you please, father ; but see him I will not, if I can possibly avoid it."

But Robert Fenwood did not come to the farm again, and Mary heard nothing of him for three weeks, during which time she never stirred out of the house. She was very unhappy, and the dreadful secret which she had learnt at the house of the colliery manager rested, as she feared it would, upon her heart like a dead weight. A dark cloud had settled upon her path, and she tried in vain to remove it. She did her household work, but her cheerful temper forsook her, and she became moody and thoughtful.

She made a strong effort at last to cast off the melancholy which was consuming her, and in this effort she was aided by the continued absence of Fenwood. He had evidently taken offence at her refusal to see him the last time he visited the farm, and would probably trouble her no more.

About six weeks had elapsed since the death of Fenwood's housekeeper, and one day Mary set out from her father's house to visit some friends at Egremont. After spending the day with them she made ready to go home. The sun had gone down before she set out on her journey, and the moon had risen. Mary felt no terror until she had left Egremont behind her; but when she reached the open country a feeling of dread stole over her, and she began to think of Robert Fenwood, of the confession of crime, and of the murder at Blaydon, until she became almost sick with fear.

"I ought not to have remained out so late," she murmured, as she hurried along the solitary road, and cast a frightened look over the dreary and barren Moor, lighted up by the rays of the moon. "Thank goodness, however, I am not so very far from home. Ah!"

She had come to a bend in the road, and the exclamation was caused by the sight of a man who suddenly confronted her. The heart of the young woman stood still for a moment, and then began to beat with fearful violence. For the moonlight, resting full upon the features, revealed to her the face of Robert Fenwood, the man whom, above all others, she would have least wished to meet at such a time and in such a place.

The colliery manager started when he heard the cry, and looked keenly into the terror-stricken countenance of her who had given utterance to it. That look told him who it was that stood before him, and he raised his hat as he said—

"Good evening, Miss Somerville. It is an unexpected pleasure to me to meet you here. I hope I see you well."

"Thank you," answered the young woman, attempting to pass him; "but it is getting late, and my father and mother will be very anxious about me. I have been to see some friends in Egremont, and I have stopped out far later than I ought to have done."

"Stay, Miss Somerville," said Fenwood, gently detaining her. "Excuse me, but I have a few words to say to you, and probably this is the best opportunity I shall have of saying them. I have never seen you since the day when poor old Ann died. Ah! she passed away very quietly from this world of sin and sorrow. I felt sadly grieved at her loss. But we must submit to every trial that our Heavenly Father chooses to impose upon us; and well will it be for us," he continued, raising his eyes to the blue sky studded with thousands of glittering stars, " if we bear them with patience and resignation. ' Whom the Lord loveth He chasteneth, and scourgeth every son whom He receiveth.' "

To hear the black-hearted scoundrel quoting Scripture and assuming an air of piety, was to the young woman more sickening than if he had uttered the most frightful curses, and she turned away from him in disgust.

" Mr Fenwood," she said, with as much firmness as she could assume, "I must go home. I have no time to-night for talking with you. If you have anything to say to me, be good enough to say it at some other time. As I have already told you, it is late, and my father and mother will be anxious about me."

A dark shade stole over the face of the colliery manager, and there was a flash of anger in the evil eyes as they rested upon her for an instant, and for an instant only.

" Miss Somerville," he said, and his voice, always disagreeable, sounded harsher than ever in the ears of the listener, " you *must* remain and hear what I have to say now."

She felt that the man who had without cause foully murdered a sick lad, and that lad his own brother, was not likely to hesitate at using violence towards herself if she provoked him, and, therefore, she determined to remain quietly where she was till he had finished, although she dreaded what was coming.

" Well, Mr. Fenwood," she said, in as light a tone as she could assume, " proceed; but be as brief as you can, and bear in mind what I have told you about my father and mother."

Apparently he did not hear her concluding words: if he did, he paid no attention to them. Standing in the centre of the road, with his eyes fixed upon the ground, Fenwood remained for some time lost in reflection. Then raising his head swiftly, he cried out, in a voice that thrilled with passion—

" Mary Somerville, I love you ! "

The young woman gave a cry of terror and dismay, and started as if she had been stung by a serpent. She was about to reply, but Fenwood stopped her.

" One moment, Miss Somerville," he cried. " Hear me to the end. When I first became acquainted with you I had never known what love was. I had heard men speak of it, but to me it appeared something in which only foolish boys and girls ought to indulge. I steeled my heart against what sentimentalists call the ' tender passion,' and determined to devote my life and powers to spreading the religion of Jesus amongst the people. I met you, and all was changed. You made me feel that there is a power in love which nothing else in the world possesses, and that where it once obtains the mastery it becomes the lord of every motion."

She was going to speak again, but he stopped her with a motion of his hand.

"I don't think," he said, speaking very slowly, and evidently under the influence of great emotion, "that you would ever have been more to me than any other woman, if your own conduct had not led me to suppose that I was not entirely indifferent to you. Forgive me for speaking so plainly, Miss Somerville; but for the avowal which I have made to-night you have only yourself to thank. Is it possible," he added—and by the light of the moon Mary saw his face grow very pale—"that you have been fooling me ?"

The thought troubled him so deeply that several minutes elapsed before he spoke again. When he did so it was with a vehemence that startled his listener.

"I will not believe it!" he exclaimed, stamping his foot violently upon the ground. "Miss Somerville," he continued, exchanging his deliberate style of speaking for a more rapid utterance. "I have told you that I love you —that I do so fervently, passionately, Heaven knows— that you yourself have encouraged this love, you will scarcely deny. I don't want you to say that you love me; but I want you to hold out a hope, that at some future day—however far distant it may be, I am content to wait —you will reward my devotion, which I here declare shall never swerve from you, by linking your fortunes with mine."

If she had not known the true character of the man, Mary Somerville would have pitied him as deeply as she condemned herself for her folly in having, for the sake of ministering to her vanity, encouraged his attentions to herself. But the thought of the foul deed in which he had been so prominent an actor rose in her mind, and she could almost fancy that she saw, by the moonlight, the face of his dead brother, wearing that awful look which it wore when he struggled for life with his murderer.

"Mr. Fenwood," she said, in a clear but trembling voice, "I have listened to you very patiently, and my answer must be very short. What I have heard from you will be treated by me as if it had never been spoken. We can never be anything more to each other than we have been—in fact, we cannot be so much. Henceforth your road in life and mine lie widely apart, and if we meet at all, we must meet as total strangers."

He staggered back as if he had received a sudden blow, and gasped for breath. Recovering himself quickly, he advanced to where she stood, and said in a low voice—

"And why?"

She never stirred, but fixed her eyes upon his with a steady gaze, in which there was not the slightest sign of fear or hesitation.

"I am not bound to answer your question," she replied.

"It is false!" he retorted fiercely. "You are bound to answer it. What!" he continued, with increasing violence, "do you think that I am a child, to be played with in this manner? I tell you that you have planned and plotted this; that you led me on the white ice, and having got me there, you now propose to desert me; that for weeks your every word, your every look, your every act were designed to impress me with the idea that you loved me as deeply and as truly as I—God help me!—love you. And when I ask you for an explanation of a change in your manner for which I am unable to account, you say that you are not bound to give it to me. Mary Somerville, beware how you provoke a desperate man. The answer which I seek from you I will have before I leave you to-night."

She drew back from him a pace or two, and raised her arm aloft, while a change passed over her face which startled him—a change which expressed all her loathing, all her dread, all her scorn of the man who stood before her.

" Walter Daneson," she said, in a voice the clear tones of which rang out upon the night air, " Remember your Brother !"

She would have given worlds, the moment the words had passed her lips, to have recalled them ; but it was too late. The murderer reeled as if struck by lightning, and a cry resembling the howl of a wild beast came from his lips. A moment afterwards he had hold of her by the arm, and she felt his hot breath upon her cheek. No need was there to ask his purpose. She read it plainly in the now hideous countenance, from which the devil flashed out ; and, in mortal terror, she screamed aloud for help.

" Oh, James Blaylock, James Blaylock," she cried, in piercing tones, " would that you were with me now !"

As if in response to her appeal, she heard a frank and manly voice saying, " Here I am ! Who calls me ?" Fenwood also heard it, for his grasp upon her arm relaxed, and as the sound of approaching footsteps became louder and more distinct, he said, in what was little more than a whisper—

"Mary Somerville, we shall meet again before long."

Then leaping over a hedge, he dashed across the Moor, and was quickly lost to view.

# CHAPTER VII.

—o—

" Come rest in this bosom, my own stricken deer ;
   Though the herd have fled from thee thy home is still here ;
   Here still is the smile that no cloud can o'ercast,
   And a heart and a hand all thy own to the last.
   Thou hast called me thy Angel in moments of bliss ;
   And thy Angel I'll be 'mid the horrors of this ;
   Through the furnace unshrinking thy steps to pursue,
   And shield thee, and save thee, or perish there too."—*Moore.*

MARY SOMERVILLE nearly fainted after Fenwood left her ; but by a strong and resolute effort she succeeded in retaining her senses, although she trembled in every limb, and could almost hear the beating of her own heart. The footsteps which she heard, and which had startled Fenwood, approached still nearer, and at length a man walking very quickly came up to the place where she stood. She uttered a cry of joy when she recognised in the new-comer James Blaylock—the man whose name had passed her quivering lips but a few moments before.

" Miss Somerville !" he said, starting back in surprise ; "is this you ? What are you doing here at this time, alone ?"

She tried to answer him, but her voice became lost in a wild hysterical burst of grief, so violent that the young man was alarmed by it.

" Be calm, Miss Somerville," he said, in a soothing tone, " and let me know how it is that I find you here at this hour, and in this condition."

Again Mary attempted to reply, but it was some time before she could do so. At last she stammered out—

"I have been stopped and insulted on my way home——"

"By whom?" interrupted the young man, quickly.

The name of Fenwood rose to the lips of Mary, but she kept it back, and was silent.

"Who was the man?" inquired James. "For man I presume it was. Where has he gone, and which direction did he take?"

The young woman pointed with her finger to the barren waste over which Fenwood had fled. James Blaylock made rapidly for the hedge which divided the Moor from the road; but, with a cry of alarm, the young woman sprang after him, and seized him by the hand.

"What are you going to do?" she asked, in a trembling voice.

"Follow the scoundrel," replied the young man, fiercely, "and thrash him within an inch of his life, if I can lay hold of him."

"No, no," she cried earnestly. "For your own sake; for—for mine, James, remain where you are. You do not know——"

Her voice died away, and she shivered from head to foot, as if with cold.

James Blaylock looked at her in amazement.

"Do you know the man?" he inquired.

"No," was the reply.

"Have you any idea who he is at all?"

"He was a stranger to me. Perhaps he was a little the worse for drink, and that made him behave as he did.

However, thanks to you, he did nothing beyond frightening me, and I have got the better of that. I think I shall reach home now without any further trouble, so I'll bid you good night, and many thanks to you for your kindness."

She wished to tell him how sincerely she had repented of her folly since that night when they last parted, and he left her in sorrow and despair. She saw him now after that parting for the first time, and as she glanced timidly at him standing beside her, there appeared to her a more dignified look in the handsome face than it had ever worn before. But there was also a coldness about his manner which made her heart sick. Would he take her at her word and leave her to proceed home alone? Had her folly and frivolity dried up the fountain of love in his breast? She asked herself these questions, and in spite of all her efforts to keep them back, the tears forced themselves into her eyes.

"I will see you home Miss Somerville," said the young man, "it would be very wrong for me to permit you to travel along this dreary road alone, short as the distance is from here to your father's house." Then noticing the tears trickling down her cheeks, he exclaimed, in an altered voice, "You are weeping, Miss Somerville! What ails you?"

She murmured some words which were inaudible, and continued to weep bitterly.

"Mary," said James Blaylock, tenderly. "do you remember the time when we last parted?"

"I do," she replied, faintly.

"Do you remember what I said to you?"

" I do."

" Ah, Mary, I have passed very many sorrowful hours since that night. I have never ceased to think about you, and I have prayed and hoped that the time would soon come when I should see you and hear from your own lips that you did not mean to wound my feelings ; that you were only jesting when you spoke as you did; and that you were convinced how sincere, how deeply, and firmly rooted is my love for you. Mary, you will not to night do as you did before—send me away from you with a heart overburdened with misery ! "

She was silent. The young man threw his arm around her waist, and said, in a voice that trembled with emotion—

" Mary, dear, I love you—God only knows how dearly ! Is my love returned ?"

She raised her beautiful face to his own, and the look which he saw there furnished a sufficient and satisfactory answer to his question.

" I do love you, James," she said, speaking rapidly, while a flush of pleasure mantled her cheeks. " I have loved you from the hour we first met, and I shall love you as long as I live. Why should I disguise my feelings ? You speak of that night when we parted. Ah, James, that parting has not caused more misery to you than it has to me. Many a time have I loathed and despised myself for my wickedness and folly ; many a time have I prayed that you would come back to me in order that I might ask your forgiveness ; many a time have I desired to be with you as I am with you now, and say to you—James, you are dearer to me than anything else on earth. I love you and you only."

In the conversation which followed it was settled that, if the consent of Mary's parents to the match could be obtained, the young couple should be married as soon as the necessary arrangements were completed. They stood talking, utterly forgetful of the lateness of the hour, until at last Mary thought of her parents, who would be waiting anxiously for her at the farm.

"Really, James," she said, "I must go home. What on earth will my father and mother think? It is shameful for me to stop out in this manner."

"Nonsense!" returned the young man. "There is nothing shameful about it. Come, let us be moving, then, as you are so uneasy. I think, Mary," he continued, as he took her arm and they set out at a brisk walk, "you must admit that there is truth in the saying,—' It is an ill wind that blows nobody good.' We should not have been as happy as we are now if that scoundrel had not stopped—Bless me! What ails you?"

She gave a low cry, and pressed her hand upon her heart. The shadow of coming evil cast itself across her path again; the recollection of Fenwood and his crime which had faded away for a time, returned, and she shuddered as she thought of his words, and the look which accompanied them—" *Mary Somerville, we shall meet again very soon.*"

"It is nothing," she replied, after a pause, during which she struggled hard to recover her composure. "I feel nervous and frightened at what has occurred to-night. It is the first time in my life that ever I was annoyed, and

I dare say it is putting me more out of the way than it ought to do."

"But you must not let it put you out of the way, Mary," said her lover. "It was lucky that I happened to come up when I did."

"God knows it was!" earnestly answered the young woman.

"Well, it was through the merest accident in the world that I happened to be astir. A friend of mine came over from Whitehaven to see me, and I accompanied him part of the way on his return home. As I came back, seeing that the night was such a fine one, I thought I would come across the Moor, and take the road leading to the left which we have just passed, in order to reach home. Coming along, and thinking of you, as I have always done ever since we first met, I heard a woman's voice calling me by name. The rest you know. Let us hope that I may be fortunate enough to find out who your assailant is, and then he and I can square accounts."

"Hush," said Mary, in terror. "Don't talk in that way. For Heaven's sake keep out of his way; avoid him as you would a serpent!"

"What!" exclaimed James, in astonishment. "You know him, then?"

"No," said Mary, confusedly. "I don't know him; but he seemed to me a dangerous man, and you know it would break my heart if any harm were to befall you. Remember," she added, in a tone which she endeavoured to render as light as possible, "you don't belong to yourself now. You are mine, and I am bound, if I can, to take care of you, and keep you out of mischief."

The reply of the young man to this speech was a very expressive one indeed. In a few minutes afterwards the pair reached the farm, and saw a light gleaming from one of the windows of the old house.

"My father and mother are in the kitchen, I think," said Mary. "I see a light burning there."

"Well, darling," said the young man, "here you are, safe and sound. So good night, and God bless you."

"You must not leave me in that way, James," said the young woman, firmly. "You must go in with me."

"Very well," was the reply; "I'll do so with pleasure."

When Mary and her lover entered the kitchen, they found Mrs. Somerville sitting on one side of the fire, engaged in what she called "mendin' a lot o' oald duds," and the farmer on the other side, smoking his pipe. He turned his head towards Mary, and said—

"Bless me, lass, woriver hes te' been till this time o' neet? We thowt thoo was lost."

"No father," replied the young woman, "I have not been lost, but I could not get home any sooner."

"Neay," replied her father, "likely nut. But whea's that wid the'?"

Mary took hold of her lover by the hand, and led him forward to where her father and mother were sitting.

"James Blaylock!" exclaimed the farmer, in surprise. "Well, this beats aw! Thoo's aboot t' last body 'at I wad ha' thowt o' seein' here."

"Ay, James Blaylock, father," said Mary; "and," she added, as the colour forsook her face, "you may thank James Blaylock that I am here at all. Had it not been for him——"

She could not finish her sentence. The dark shadow fell upon her path again.

" What's been t' matter ?" inquired the farmer, after a pause.

" A blackguard that Mary met with in coming home stopped and insulted her," said the young man, speaking for his sweetheart. "I chanced, very luckily, to be going along the road at the time, and when he heard me he made off across the Moor. It was well for him that he did so," added the speaker, in a low determined voice, " for if I could only have laid hold of him I would have broken every bone in his cowardly carcase."

" Whea was it, Mary ?" said the farmer, turning to his daughter.

" I—I don't know, father," she replied, almost inaudibly.

" Well, it's a gud job nowt's neay warse," said Richard Somerville. " An' James, me lad," he continued, addressing the young man. " I'se for iver obleeged tull the', an' seay is t' mistriss. I allus hed a gud opinion on the', an' I've said aback o' the' back what I'se gahn to say afooar the' feace—that theear isn't a stiddier, quieter, nor nicer yung fellow to be fund on Cleator Moor."

" I am very glad you think so, father," said Mary, smiling and brightening up.

" Is te' ?"

" Yes."

" What for ?"

" Because your opinion so entirely coincides with my own."

F

" Varra glad to hear it. But when did te' git in that way o' thinkin' ?"

" I have been in that way of thinking for some time."

" Hoo lang ?"

" Ever since James and I first met."

" Ay !" muttered the farmer ; " a body wad hardly ha' thowt seay though, widoot thoo'd tell't them theesel'."

" And to-night," said Mary, blushing, " I have given a proof of my opinion about him, for he has asked me to become his wife, and I have consented to do so—that is, if you have no objection."

The farmer dropped his pipe and sat staring, first at his daughter and then at her lover, in blank astonishment. Mrs. Somerville, with an exclamation, let fall her sewing, and rose from her seat.

" You seem surprised, father," said Mary.

" Well, I is, rayder," said the farmer, drily. " But what hes James to say aboot it ?"

" I have this to say, Mr. Somerville," replied the young man, his handsome face flushed with excitement. " I love Mary, and am proud and happy to know that she loves me. To-night she has consented, if you and her mother are willing, to marry me ; and, God helping me, it will be the study of my life so to treat her, that she shall never rue the hour when she expressed herself ready to unite her fate with mine. I could say a great deal more, but any language that was ever written or spoken would convey to you a very poor idea of my feelings."

" And, Mary," said the farmer, in a low voice, and with trembling lips, " what does thoo say aboot it, me lass ?"

" Father," said the young woman, falling on her knees and raising her clasped hands towards him, " my dear father, I love James, I have always loved him, and I loved him the best when I treated him with the greatest coldness. Like you and my mother he has overlooked my folly in the past—for which I am truly penitent—and I will try to atone for any injustice I may have done to him by devoting my life to the promotion of his happiness. And now, father, mother, bless us both. James, kneel down beside me. God grant that the darkness which has hung over me so long may be removed, and that the sun may shine out brightly in the future."

James Blaylock knelt down close to the young woman ; and father and mother earnestly invoked the Divine blessing upon the wedded life of the young pair. Then falling on his knees, while his wife also assumed an attitude of devotion, Richard Somerville offered up a prayer to the Great Father who watches tenderly over the meanest and poorest of His creatures, and whose love for them is more lasting than the stars He made, which have held on their course since the creation of the world.

It was close upon midnight when James Blaylock left the farm and wended his way homewards, as happy a man as could have been found in the dominions of the king.

And Mary—what of her ? She desired to be alone, that she might think leisurely over the occurrences of that eventful night. So, after the departure of her lover, she quickly sought the solitude of her own apartment, and there with her head resting upon her hand, sat for a long time reflecting upon what had taken place. In the excitement, caused by her meeting with James Blaylock, her dread and horror of Fenwood had been partially, although not wholly, swallowed up. But that dread and horror now returned with increased force. She bitterly rued the indiscretion of which she had been guilty in letting him know that she was acquainted with his dreadful secret, and she thought with a shudder of the effect which that knowledge had produced upon him, and his parting words. That she had converted him into an enemy there could not be the slightest doubt; and an enemy so violent and unscrupulous as he was, was capable of going to any length in order to gratify his revenge. Again the idea recurred to her mind of making his crime known to her friends, and delivering him up to justice; and again she abandoned it. How was she to prove her statement if she charged him with the crime of murder? The manuscript which she had read, and which he had been imprudent enough to leave exposed, he would, if he had not previously done so, doubtless destroy upon his return home that night. Where, then, was the evidence of his guilt to come from? No; it would never do for her to take the rash step of having him arrested, although it was to be regretted that the sin which he had committed should pass unpunished. After all, his parting words might only be an idle threat, and what she had told him that night might have the effect of making him avoid her. And then, she had secured a brave defender in James Blaylock—a defender who would willingly lay down his life for her sake. So she reasoned; and at last, completely wearied, laid down to rest with the name of her lover upon her lips.

When she awoke the following morning, the rays of the sun were streaming through the window into her room.

On reaching the kitchen she found her mother sitting alone, and was told that her father had gone out into the fields. After taking breakfast, the young woman was about to rise from the table, when the door opened, and Mr. James Jenkins entered the apartment.

" Gud mornin', Jimmy," said Mrs. Somerville. " Cum in an' sit doon, min, an' tell us hoo thoo's gitten on."

Mr Jenkins, looking more comical than ever, complied with the request. Having placed his hat carefully upon a table, he turned quickly upon Mrs. Somerville, and said in a sharp tone—

" I'll tell yé what, Mrs. Sumerville, I've heerd fwok say 'at t' divil's barnes hes their deddy's luck; an' if that be sooa, I mun be a saint, for theear niver was a pooar fellow so harrish'd as I've been leately."

" What's t' matter noo, Jimmy ?" inquired Mrs. Somerville.

" What's t' matter !" echoed Jenkins. " Matter annuff ! Bless me heart, it's a wunder I hevn't gon clean crazy lang sen ! I tell't yé t' last time I was here hoo me an' t' wife was bodder'd wid them lads. Wey, woman, sen that they've been ten times war nor iver. What do yé think they did tudder neet ? They emptied a bucketful o' watter anunder t' dooar when I was sitten at me supper, an' t' pleace was aw of a swum derectly. Thinks I, I'll give sum on yé hot coffee, an' I jump't off me chair an' ron till t' dooar. I heerd sum on them scuddin' away as if Oald Harry was efter them, an' when I gat ootside theear was nobbet yan on them left. I duddent see whea it was, but I saw it was a man, an' he seemed as if he was mackin' for oor hoose. ' Bad luck till the', thoo midneet disturber, says I, ' tak that ! ' an' I hit him reet atween t' eyes wid me fist. He tummel't as if he'd been shot, an' shootit ten thoosand murders. I varra nar lost me senses when I heerd t' voice. For whea div ye think it was ? T' seame time 'at t' scamps emptied t' watter anunder my dooar, sum o' their gang hed emptied anudder bucketful anunder oald Flanigan's dooar, 'at tudder side o' t' road. T' oald fellow com oot like mesel' to see whea it was that hed dun it, an' when he saw me he mead ower to speak till me. But afooar he cud git a wurd oot I gev him a pair of as bonny black eyes as iver yé saw i' your life."

" Oh, dear ! " cried Mrs. Somerville. " What a pity ! "

" Ay," returned Jenkins, with a melancholy shake of the head, " yé may weel say that. But yé hevn't heerd t' warst on it yit. For me life I cuddent persuade t' oald hawfthick that I hedn't dun it o' purpose, an' he swore be t' piper that played afooar Moses an' ' Saint Proggins' that he wad tak me afooar t' magistrates at Whitehebben. An' sure annuf he went t' next day to Whitehebben an' gat a summins. When I com till t' hoose, I thowt t' wife wad ha' tyan leeve o' her wits. ' Noo, thoo hes dun it,' says she. ' Dun what ? ' says I. ' Dun what, thoo maizlin ! ' says she ; ' I wad think a sham o' mesel', min, to gang an' strike at an oald man.' ' I struck at him be mistak,' says I. ' Did te ? ' says she. 'Ay, than, they'll mebbe send the' to jail be mistak, an' t' ya mistak 'll stand agean tudder.' ' Well, that is nice consolation,' says I. ' Thoo is yan o' Job's comforters, sartenly. But what is I to dui ? ' says I. ' Gang ower to Flanigan, an' try to mak it up wid him,' says t' wife. ' I wad as suin try to mak it up wid a Bunghole tiger,' says I. 'If I went inside his dooar, Kitty—that's his wife—wad throw fire in me feace.'"

# CHAPTER VIII.

—o—

"But time at last brings all things even;
  And if we do but wait the hour,
  There never yet was human power
That could evade, if unforgiven,
  The patient watch and vigils long
  Of him who treasures up a wrong."—*Byron.*

"WELL, than," continued Mr. Jenkins, proceeding with his narrative, "when t' wife fund 'at I waddent gang ower to Flanigan's, she says, 'Thoo'd better gang to Whitehebben, an' speak till a lawyer.' 'Whea is I to gang tull?' says I. 'Misther Swivel,' says she. 'Misther Swivel!' I says, 'that's a queer neame.' 'Ay,' says she, 'an' he's a queer fellow 'at it belangs till. But, dui as I tell the'. His offish is in Queen Street, an' queer as he is, he's clever, and mebbe he'll help the' oot o' t' hobble 'at thoo's been daft annuff to git intil.' Neay suiner said than dun. I set off to Whitehebben, fund t' offish, and knock'd at t' dooar. A lantern-jaw't lad in a jacket oppen't it, an' I says tull him, 'Is Misther Swivel in?' He luikt at me fray heid to fut, and than he says, 'Yes; do you want to see him?' 'To be sure I div,' says I. 'What do you want with him?' says he. 'What's that to thee, thoo snafflin' yap? Does te' think 'at I hev neay mair sense than tell thee me bisness?' Well, t' creatur glower't at me, an' than he girn't; efter that he went inside, an' com oot agean, an' says, 'Walk this way.' I follow't in, an' he show't me

intil a room, wor a lal wizen't oald fellow was sitten wid a
pair o' specks on. 'Do you want to see me?' says he,
quite sharp like. 'Ur yé Misther Swivel?' says I.
'That's my name,' says he; 'what do you want?' 'I've
cum to ax your advice,' says I. 'What about,' says he.
'Well,' says I, 'suppose yé wor a daft oald Irishman,
leevin' aside o' me, an' iv a dark neet I was to happen, in
a mistak, to draw me fist an' blacken yér silly oald een,
div yé think t' magistrates wad dui owt till me for it? If
they did they wad be a bonny lot o' gammerstangs.' Well,
if ye'll believe me, Mistriss Sumerville, t' article hardly
gev me time to finish till he jump't off his seat wid a feace
as white as a dishclout, a' meade for t' dooar. When he
reach't it an' oppen't it, he bawls oot, 'John, show this
blackguard out of the place.' 'Blaggard!' says I; 'yé
oald newdles, whea ur yé cawin' a blaggard? Is this yer
thenks for givin' yé me custom?' He niver minded me,
but keep't shootin' 'John, John!' an' at last t' lantern-
jaw't lad com intil t' room. 'Show this man out,' says t'
lal chap. 'This way, sir,' says t' lad. I'd hafe a notion
o' knockin' t' oald fellow on his back, but thinks I, I've got
mesel' intil ya scrape, an' in tryin' to git oot on't I'se gahn
to git intil anudder if I divn't mind what I'se aboot; seay
I follow't t' lad quietly. He oppen't t' street dooar, an'
afooar I knew wor I was, he gev me a pick that sent me
fleein' heid furst intil t' middle o' t' peavement, an' than
ron in. But that wasn't t' warst o' t' job. Efter I'd been
theear, oald Flanigan went an' hir't t' lawyer to appear
agean me; an' when I show't mesel' afooar t' magistrates,
that oald fellow caw't me war nor if I'd been a pickpocket.
I thowt yance ower they wor gahn to send me to jail; but,

hooiver, I gat off as many a better fellow's gitten off—wid payin'. Noo, I want to ax yé honestly, Mistriss Sumerville, did yé iver hear o' seck an unfortinat divil as me?'"

"Thoo reely is varra unlucky, Jimmy," said Mrs. Somerville, smiling.

"Eh, dear!" said Mr. Jenkins, with a doleful look. "It's terrible wark. But I'se at me oald trade agean. I've talk't that much aboot mesel', that I have forgitten me errand. Hev yé heerd t' news?"

"What news?" inquired Mrs. Somerville.

"Wey, aboot Misther Fenwood."

Mary started, and her face flushed and then paled as she looked earnestly at the speaker.

"No, we've heerd nowt aboot him," replied Mrs. Somerville. What's to dee wid him?"

"I thowt yé wad ha' known," said Mr. Jenkins; and then he continued, apparently unconscious that he was making himself ridiculous, "I thowt yé waddent know, so I've cum't to tell yé."

"Tell us what?" asked Mrs. Somerville.

"Well, they say that Misther Fenwood's tyan a fit, or summat o' that kind, an' he's nobbet in a varra queer way."

"Bless us!" said Mrs. Somerville. "Hoo did that happen?"

"Can't tell hoo it happen't," replied Mr. Jenkins; "but as far as I can larn, his hoosekeeper didn't hear him astur this mornin', an' as he niver offer'd to cum doonstairs, she went up till his bedroom, an' i' steed o' seeing him i' bed, she fund him liggen on t' flooar, bleedin' at mooth and nose like a stuck pig. Hoo lang he'd laid theear, gudness only knows."

"Dear me, dear me!" exclaimed Mrs. Somerville. "An' is he nut likely to git better?"

"Yis, I think he is," replied Jenkins. "They sent for a doctor, an' t' doctor said 'at he wad hev to be varra careful, or it wad gang hard wid him; but if he nobbet minded hissel', he med cum roond agean. Hooiver, I mun be off to me wark, Mistriss Sumerville. I've stopt here far ower lang, so I'll bid yé gud mornin'."

"Gud mornin', Jemmy," replied Mrs. Somerville. "My gudness!" she proceeded, after the village gossip had left the house, "but it is a bad job aboot Mr. Fenwood. Whativer can be t' matter wid him?"

Mary was silent, but she knew the cause of Fenwood's illness. There could be little doubt that the tremendous blow she had dealt him the previous night, when she called him by his right name, and convinced him that the knowledge of his crime was no longer confined to himself, had produced the physical prostration from which he was suffering. She would have pitied him, but for the fact that for the murder of his brother there was not, according to his own statement, the shadow of an excuse. It was a foul inhuman, cowardly act, done without the slightest provocation, and it stamped its perpetrator as a disgrace to humanity. She hoped, however, that if he should recover from the illness under which he was labouring, he would leave Cleator Moor. Indeed, it was very probable that he would do so, seeing that it would be unsafe for him to remain in a neighbourhood where one person, at least, was acquainted with his antecedents and might reveal them at any moment. Mary Somerville dwelt upon this idea with considerable satisfaction, and the more she dwelt upon it, the more her fear of Fenwood began to diminish.

The weeks rolled rapidly away, and the young woman became once more cheerful and happy, and the light and life of her father's household. Occasionally she would give way to fits of despondency, and the dreadful secret which she had found out in such a remarkable manner at times oppressed her mind; but these fits were not of long duration : she got rid of them as fast as possible, and did her best to blot out from her recollection all thoughts of Fenwood and his terrible crime.

A month had elapsed since that night when they parted on the road under the circumstances described in a previous chapter. Mary heard occasionally, from visitors, that Fenwood was rapidly recovering, although he had not, since he was attacked with illness, left his house. James Blaylock was a nightly visitor at the farm; the day of his marriage with Mary had been fixed, and all the necessary preparations for that important and happy event were being made. Matters were in this state when a young woman, named Ruth Grayson, the daughter of a well-to-do yeoman in the neighbourhood, called upon Mary one evening. Miss Grayson was a tall and rather stout young lady, with a very pleasant face, very red cheeks, and very bright black eyes, and, taken altogether, she was what a celebrated domestic critic, once writing of a beautiful actress, called " an eminently gatherable-to-one's-arms sort of person."

"My dear Mary" said this young lady—whose cheeks were redder than usual with brisk walking, and who talked very fast—"how are you getting on? It's an age since I saw you. But I haven't had the chance of seeing you, for I've been burried alive with two old aunts at Workington during the last four or five months, and I only got home a few days ago. But I'll tell you what I've called about. There's to be a party at Whitehaven to-morrow afternoon, given by Mrs. Jackson, an old acquaintance of mine, who got married a short time ago—the more fool she, say I, for making herself the slave of any man."

"It does not follow," said Mary, smiling, "that because a woman marries a man she should become his slave."

"Oh, doesn't it, though?" said Miss Grayson, tossing her head disdainfully. "Well, you see, your opinion and mine differ very much upon that point. But, as I was saying, she's going to give a party, and she's invited me to attend it and take three or four friends with me. I've got three—Jane Glaister, Harriet Ware, and Mary Beck—to go with me; and I want you to make the fourth. You'll go, won't you?

"I really cannot say," was the reply. "I don't know whether I can spare the time."

"Ah! I know you are going to get married," retorted Miss Grayson; "and you'll be kept very busy just now. There, you needn't blush. Bless you, its no secret; and I may tell you this—that if I had not formed a resolution to keep the men—wretches that they are—at a proper distance, and never on any account to sacrifice my liberty, I should certainly have set my cap at your intended."

"Would you indeed?" said Mary.

" That I should," retorted Miss Grayson. " There ; I
see you are very grateful to me for not doing it, but I don't
require any thanks. I shall be quite satisfied if you will
consent to form one of our party."

Mary reflected for a little while, and then said—

" Well, I don't mind if I do go with you."

" That's a good girl," replied Miss Grayson. " Now,
suppose you come over to our house after dinner to-morrow.
All the other girls will be there, and we can proceed to
Whitehaven together, and return home in company."

" That arrangement will suit me admirably," said Mary.

Miss Grayson then took her departure. After she had
left, Mary acquainted her father and mother with the
engagement which she had made. Neither of them raised
the slightest objection to it.

Mary did not see James Blaylock that night. He had
left Cleator Moor for Maryport at the commencement of
the week to transact some business, and was not expected
to return until the following evening.

The next day, after dinner, the young woman, with a
promise to return home that night as soon as she could,
proceeded to the residence of Ruth Grayson. On her
arrival there, she found that young lady and her friends
ready to set out with her to Whitehaven.

The day was not a pleasant one. The sun had taken
a holiday, and a gloom rested upon everything. The wind
was keen and cold, and swept over the Moor in gusts, with
a moaning mournful sound. It was one of those days
when nervous, unhappy men think of suicide, when the
the spirits of the light-hearted are depressed, when mothers
become cross and think everything a trouble, and when

even a cloud settles upon the bright faces of children at play. The country, bleak and desolate always in that wild region, looked on that day more bleak and desolate than ever, and the summits of the mountains in the distance were enveloped in mist.

The night was closing in, and the moon had risen, when a man, carrying a stick in his hand and a basket slung over his arm, left Cleator Moor for Whitehaven. Few persons would have thought, if they had seen him walking along the road, that he was totally blind, and yet such was the case ; for the traveller was none other than Charles Loftus, the blind pedlar, to whom the reader was introduced shortly after the commencement of our tale.

With as bold and fearless a step as if it had been noon-day, and he had possessed the faculty of which he was deprived, the pedlar proceeded on his journey. The still-ness which prevailed was unbroken by a single sound except the moaning of the wind as it swept over the Moor. Cleator Moor lay about half-a-mile behind the pedlar, and he had reached a very lonely place, where a hedge on one side divided the road from a barren tract of land ; whilst on the other side, fenced off from the highway, was a deep stone quarry. It was here that the pedlar, walking at a rapid rate, stumbled over a large stone lying in his way, and fell heavily to the ground.

The fall was so violent that he was almost rendered senseless by it, and he remained for several minutes groaning with pain, and unable to move.

"I believe I have lamed myself," he murmured. " What am I to do ? Walk back to any of the houses and ask them to take me in I cannot, and to go forward is equally out of the question. If I could only manage to get to the side of the road and rest for about an hour, perhaps I might be able to resume my journey homewards. Thank God," he continued, raising himself with considerable difficulty to a sitting position, "I have not broken any bones; but I am certain that I cannot walk at present. Whereabouts am I? As nearly as I can calculate, Steadman's Quarry is close at hand on my right. If that be so, there is an opening in the fence on the left through which I can creep, and lie down in the field for a short time. The grass is damp, I dare say; but at all events it is preferable in my condition to lying on this hard road."

He tried to rise to his feet, but fell back suddenly with a low moan. After a short rest, the injured man roused himself again, and grasping his stick and basket, commenced to creep very slowly and painfully towards that side of the highway which was separated from the adjoining land. As easily as if he had seen it, the pedlar found the opening he had referred to, which was large enough to admit of the passage of a man. Creeping though it, and taking his stick and stock-in-trade with him, Loftus threw himself down wearily upon the grass.

There for the present let us leave him, and return to Mary Somerville.

The young woman spent a pleasant afternoon at Whitehaven, and it was about nine o'clock when she left that town with her companions for home. Mary Somerville had never been happier than she was that night. Miss Grayson's married friend had received and treated her very kindly; and the time, spent in the congenial society of young persons in her own station of life, had passed so rapidly that she was surprised when she glanced at the clock and saw that the evening was so far advanced. The five young ladies, after passing through Hensingham, beguiled the time by singing snatches of songs in concert, and their musical voices, rising clearly upon the night air, could not have failed to charm the most flinty-hearted old bachelor that ever lived, had he but heard them.

"Goodness gracious!" said Mary, at the conclusion of one of the songs, "what on earth can we be thinking about? Here we are, singing upon the highway like a set of benighted topers, instead of walking soberly and modestly home, like respectable young ladies returning from a respectable party. Upon my word, I am ashamed of you."

"Indeed!" retorted Miss Grayson, sharply. "Do you think, while you are about it, that you could not manage to be ashamed of yourself—just a very little bit?"

"I am ashamed of myself," said Mary, with a light-hearted laugh; "not a very little bit, but a very great deal."

"Ah," said Miss Grayson, "I believe you. You're a sincere penitent, evidently. Well, for my part, I would sooner travel on a road with a light heart and a clear conscience, singing a good song, young woman as I am, than I would pull a face as long as a fiddle, and pretend to be a saint with, at the same time, as little of the saint about me as there is about a Tug."

"A Tug!" repeated Miss Ware. "What in the world is that?"

"Why," responded Miss Grayson, "it's an Indian, whose religion consists in choking people."

G

" You mean Thug," said Mary.

" Do I ?" retorted Ruth. " Well I am glad of it, because as long as you know my meaning, there is no necessity for me to explain myself further. But whether it's ' Tug ' or ' Thug ' doesn't matter much ; what I mean to say is that we should none of us be other than what we seem. I'll tell you what," continued Miss Grayson, warming with her subject, and speaking with great energy, " if there is one person that I hate worse than another, it is a hypocrite—a canting, snivelling, good-for-nothing, that looks as if butter wouldn't melt in his mouth, and yet cheese wouldn't choke him. "

By this time the party had reached a point about a mile distant from Cleator Moor, where a road branched off to the right.

" Here we must separate," said Ruth. " My nearest way home, and that of Harriet, Jane, and Mary, lies this way "—pointing with her finger to the road already mentioned. " You, Mary, have to keep straight on by yourself. If you are afraid of going home alone, we will keep you company ; it will only be a walk round for us."

" Thank you," said Mary ; I can find my way by myself, and I am not at all afraid of travelling alone. What a beautiful night it is !"

The sky was studded with glittering stars, and the moon, which was at the full, riding in stately beauty over the clouds, seemed like a silver lamp suspended in the vault of heaven. A lovely night had succeeded to a gloomy day, and mountain and moor were bathed in a flood of silver.

Mary took leave of her four companions, and went down
the road to the right, and she heard them laughing
merrily and singing until the sound of their voices died
away in the distance. Then a strange fear crept over her
—a foreboding of coming evil—and she felt inclined to run
after the young women and request them to turn back and
accompany her to her father's house. But the dread of
being laughed at and ridiculed restrained her, and she
abandoned the notion almost as soon as it was formed.

Notwithstanding the splendour of the evening, the wind
still continued to sweep in cold blasts over the Moor, and
it struck a chill to the heart of Mary Somerville as she
stood gazing earnestly and anxiously in the direction
where her friends had disappeared. She stood thus,
motionless and thoughtful for a considerable time, and
then with a sigh went forward towards her home.

All her gaiety and light-heartedness had suddenly left
her—it had disappeared with the young women who had
just parted from her—and thoughts which she would have
given the wealth of an empire to banish for ever took
possession of her mind. They were gloomy thoughts,
arising out of and connected with the events of the last
few months, with which she had had so much to do.

Mary pursued her journey with a rapid step until she
was about a hundred and fifty yards from Steadman's
Quarry, and then a man, who had evidently been con-
cealing himself, came quickly from the hedge, and stood
right before her. The young woman gave one single look
at the face, and sprang backwards with a cry of
terror. For by the light of the moon which rested upon

the features—distorted and made positively hideous by hatred and passion—she saw that the man who barred her passage was Robert Fenwood.

# CHAPTER IX.

—o—

"Two sudden blows with a ragged stick,
    And one with a heavy stone,
A sudden gash with a hasty knife,
    And then the deed was done.
There was nothing lying at my feet,
    But lifeless flesh and bone."
                *The Dream of Eugene Aram, by Hood.*

FENWOOD stood with folded arms, looking at the young woman, and a smile of mingled mockery and triumph passed over his face. Mary Somerville was almost paralysed by the sight of this man, whom she hated and feared so much, rising up suddenly in her path like a spirit of evil, and her hurried breathing and death-like countenance told how great was the dread which possessed her.

"Good evening, Mary Somerville," he said at last, breaking the silence—and his harsh voice, with its Northumbrian burr, sounded more harshly in her ears then it had ever done before—"I am glad to see you. You remember my words when last we parted. I told you then that we should meet again before long. Those words have come true."

The young woman made an effort to speak, but only succeeded in uttering an inarticulate murmur. She looked around her in helpless, hopeless agony, far from all assistance, alone with a man whose fierce passions she had roused, and whose guilty soul was stained with the crime of murder. She would have fled from him if she had had the power, but her feet seemed nailed to the place where she stood. This thought of hers he evidently divined, for he said in a sarcastic tone—

"You need not attempt to escape from me, for the attempt would be useless. And we are not likely to be interrupted to-night. You wish to know, doubtless, how it is that I am here. Well, it is only fair that I should tell you."

Mary continued silent, simply because the power of speech had for the time deserted her. Indeed, so fixed and motionless was she, that but for her rapid breathing and a slight movement of the head, it might have been thought the sight of Fenwood had turned her into stone. But she fastened a steady look upon his face, and his evil eyes began to wander when he saw that hers were bent upon him. A few moments passed before he spoke again.

"I was saying that you would doubtless wish to know how it is that I am here," he at length proceeded. "After I left you on that night when, in a few words, you told me that you had availed yourself of a visit to my house in order to pry into the history of my past life, I was seized, as you have probably heard, with a dangerous illness. For a fortnight I lay hovering between life and death, bu. my will was stronger than the disease which attacked met I was determined to live for revenge! Unknown to you, I have kept myself informed of all your movements. I learnt this morning of your intended visit to Whitehaven. This afternoon I sent my housekeeper away to see her friends, and requested her to return to-morrow or the day following. To-night I left my house alone and unobserved, and for the first time since you told me that you—that I had—in short——"

He broke off in confusion; and turned very pale. Mary had by this time somewhat recovered her self-possession, although she was still very much agitated. She saw that there was nothing to be gained by striving to conciliate the wretch who stood before her, and she thought that, bad as he was, for his own sake he would not dare to offer her personal violence.

"Let me commence where you left off," she said, speaking in a clear and deliberate voice. "You left your house for the first time since I told you that your name was not Robert Fenwood, but Walter Daneson, and that you were the murderer of your brother."

He made one step towards her, his face convulsed with passion; but she stood firm, and looked at him with a fearless unflinching gaze. As suddenly as he had advanced he retreated again, and tried hard, apparently, to keep down the rage which was almost choking him.

"You are imprudent," he said, and his white lips quivered as he spoke; "but that matters little. Yes," he continued, with savage energy, raising his clenched hand aloft, "my name is Walter Daneson, and I am the murderer of my brother—a second Cain, if you will, only there is no brand upon my brow."

The last words were spoken in a tone of such bitter mockery, that the horror-stricken hearer of them shuddered from head to foot.

"God have mercy upon me!" she murmured. "This is dreadful. And to think that a wretch like this has dared, day after day, and week after week, to take Thy Holy Name in vain, and make a mockery of Thy religion!"

"Dared!" repeated Fenwood—as we shall continue to call him—"What is it that a man like me dare not do? Mary Somerville you talk like a child. I have made a mockery of religion, have I? Well, that is only what thousands of men and women do every day. The grocer who sands his sugar and adulterates his flour; the draper who sells the same quality of cloth for different prices; the tradesmen who cheat their customers, and go to church on the Sunday because it looks respectable, what do they do but make a mockery of religion? I joined a body of Dissenters and became one of their preachers, simply because it gave me a certain standing which I rather liked, and also because I felt a pleasure in seeing how easily a lot of people —your own father amongst the number—could be duped into the belief that I, Walter Daneson, stood but a little lower than the angels."

He burst out laughing as he concluded, but there was something in the laugh which froze the blood in the veins of his listener.

"I will not remain one moment longer," she exclaimed, in a determined and indignant tone, "to listen to such horrid blasphemy. Your allusion to my father is dastardly and mean. You deceived him, it is true; but a word from me would have revealed your real character to him, and that word would have been spoken had not pity—mistaken pity, I see clearly now—for your wretched self restrained me. Stand aside, sir, and let me pass."

He nevered stirred. Thoroughly aroused, Mary went to the side of the road, with a view of getting beyond him;

but he stepped in front of her, and said in a low voice—

"You cannot pass. I have something more to say to you, and I will not permit you to leave me."

"Do you dare," said the young woman, with flashing eyes, "to keep me here against my will?"

He made no answer.

"Once more," she continued, "I ask you to stand aside and let me pass. If you persist in detaining me, I will call out for assistance."

"Call out as loud as you like," said Fenwood, indicating with his hand the silent and deserted Moor. "Who is to assist you here? You cannot expect a miracle to be wrought in your favour twice in the same year. And it was only by a miracle, or something very like it, that our last interview was interrupted. We two are utterly alone. Look around, and see if you can see any one. Listen; can you hear a single sound?"

He spoke truly, Mary felt, when he said that they were alone. There was no sound save the moaning of the wind as it swept mournfully past them.

"Mary Somerville," he proceeded, "we have wasted a great deal of time in useless talk. Let us come at once to the point. What does the woman deserve who, when she obtains admission into a house, takes advantage of the absence and confidence of its owner to play the part of a spy, to pry into secrets which don't concern her, to read documents which were never intended either for her eyes or those of any other person but the writer's, and who is then base enough to fling in his teeth her knowledge of a deed obtained by such vile means?"

She was about to speak, but he stopped her with a motion of his hand.

" What does the woman deserve," he continued, and his voice trembled with passion, " who to please her fancy, and for no other purpose, wins the affections of a man, who entraps him by scheming as contemptible as it is heartless, and who, having succeeded in her despicable object, flings him to one side like a broken toy ? "

Ah, never were the pangs of self-reproach for her thoughtless conduct so keen in the breast of Mary Somerville as they were at that moment ! She could not but acknowledge to herself that the accusations brought against her by Fenwood were true.

" Look at me," he went on, striking his breast with his clenched hand. " I am Walter Daneson, the man who yielded to the temptation of the devil and slew his brother, his innocent, gentle, kind-hearted, unoffending brother : but have I ever injured you ? Was it for your sake that I first visited the house of your father ? Did I cast myself in your way, and by guile, and deceit, and hypocrisy lead you to believe that I loved you ? Have I tried to penetrate the history of your past life ? Hypocrite and villain as I am, have I ever at any time done you wrong ? "

" Mr Daneson, or Fenwood," faltered Mary, " I know that I have done wrong. I have been weak and sinful, and God is my witness how earnestly and sincerely I have repented, and still repent, of my folly. That I had no right to pry into your secrets I admit ; that I played a shameful and a sorry part in reading that which was not intended for me, I shall not attempt to deny ; but I declare to you, solemnly, that not a single word has ever passed my lips concerning what I read, except to yourself when I saw you last, and what I said then was uttered in a hasty and ungarded moment."

The features of Fenwood relaxed into a grim smile.

"With regard to your second charge," said Mary, "I feel, God knows how bitterly, that there is a great deal of truth in it ; and if I have wronged you in any way, I crave your forgiveness. Surely, Mr. Fenwood, you are not altogether bad—your heart is not altogether seared! I know that these things are hard to bear ; but try and overlook the folly of a silly girl—pardon me for having, in a moment of vanity, pretended to be animated by a feeling which had no place in my breast—and I pledge you my word, in return, that the secret of your life shall never be divulged by me to mortal. Let us separate now and for ever ; and if you will take my advice, you will leave Cleator Moor, for I am sure it must be very distasteful to you—throw off the cloak of hypocrisy, which you have worn too long—and endeavour by a life of penitence and prayer, offered up from a humble and contrite heart, to atone for the past."

"You talk well, Miss Somerville," he retorted, in a sardonic tone, "but all your talking will not move me from my purpose."

"I have talked to you too long," replied Mary, indignantly, "and it is plain that I have been wasting my time. Mr. Daneson, or Fenwood—I scarcely know which to call you—once more I ask you to let me proceed homewards. Under any circumstances, it would not be fitting that I should stand here talking with you at this hour ;

still less is it fitting that I should do so, when I have engaged to become the wife of James Blaylock."

" The wife of James Blaylock," cried Fenwood, with a
horrid laugh. " No, no, Mary Somerville ; you are mistaken. It is not likely that you will ever become the wife
of James Blaylock, or of any other man."

Like lightning, the awful danger in which she stood
flashed across the mind of the young woman, and with
parted lips and trembling limbs she waited for what was
to follow."

" Do you think," said Fenwood—and the words came
from between his teeth in a hissing whisper—" that I am
fool enough to permit you to leave me—knowing what you
know—when I have you completely in my power ? Do
you fancy that your soft speeches will move me ? When
we last separated, I vowed that I would be revenged upon
you ; when my senses returned after I was struck down
by illness, caused by what you told me that night, I
thought only of revenge. For days I have hoped for it,
dreamt of it, prayed for it, and at last the time has arrived
when I can take it. MARY SOMERVILLE, YOU MUST DIE ! "

With a low cry and in an agony of fear, she threw herself on her knees before him, and clasped her hands tightly
together. There was a beseeching look in the white face
that would have melted the heart of any one possessing
the least spark of humanity ; but Fenwood had nothing
human about him except the form.

" Mr Fenwood," she gasped, " you cannot mean what
you say. For God's sake spare my life. I am young,
and oh ! it is hard to die at my age and leave the world.
Let me go—for heaven's sake let me go—and I will never

breathe a syllable of what has occurred this night to any one. Do not—for your own soul's sake—commit this second crime! Keep back!" she cried, her voice rising to a shriek, and springing to her feet as she saw him moving towards her. " Help! Mur——"

Her voice died away under the clutch of the hand which seized her by the throat with a grasp of iron. The poor girl made a feeble effort to release herself from the hold which was choking out her life ; but she was like a child in the grip of a giant. The beautiful face turned black, and the eyes seemed as if they were about to start from their sockets ; but the murderer remorselessly tightened his grasp, growling at the same time like a wild beast. At last the struggles of the helpless victim ceased. Fenwood released his hold upon her, and she fell to the ground—a corpse!

Yes, Mary Somerville was dead. She who had left home that morning a happy, light-hearted young woman, thinking of her intended husband and of the bright future which lay before her—she who had been the pride of her poor old father's heart and the idol of her doting mother— she whose faults were in a great measure due to her careless training, but whose virtues far outbalanced her defects —she whose merry laugh and cheerful voice had made a paradise of home—was dead. The warm, loving, noble heart had ceased to beat for ever, and the face so beautiful in life was hideous now.

The murderer stood looking at his victim for a short time with his arms crossed, and, vile and wicked as he was, a feeling of awe stole over him. It has been truly said that there is a majesty in death which is denied to the living, and the beggar in his shroud inspires more reverence than the king upon his throne. Not that Fenwood felt any remorse for the abominable crime which he had perpetrated. He experienced no pity for the fate of her, the thread of whose life he had severed when that life was at its brightest. If the vital spark could have animated that fair form once again, he would have ruthlessly quenched it. But despite his hardened and devilish nature, the thought that she who but a few brief moments before had stood in his presence a living, breathing woman, full of health and vigour, had passed away for ever, caused a thrill to pass through his frame which he had never felt before, save when he stood by the bed on which his murdered brother lay.

The feeling of awe, however, suddenly gave place to one of terror lest he should be found by some one standing beside the dead body. So far, everything had been in his favour, and he might go away and leave the corpse lying where it had fallen, without any danger to himself. For no human eye had beheld the struggle which ended in the death of Mary Somerville; no one had seen their meeting; no one had heard their conversation. But it was difficult to say what might happen. If the corpse, with the marks of violence upon it, should be found upon the road, an inquiry would be set on foot which might, despite every precaution, lead to very unpleasant results, to say the least of it. These thoughts passed in quick succession through the mind of Fenwood, and he at once decided upon his course of action.

He stooped down and lifted the dead and still warm body of the young woman from the ground. A shudder convulsed his strong frame from head to foot as he looked in the distorted face. He went swiftly along the highway with his burden until he reached the fence beside the stone quarry already mentioned. Carefully lowering the body to the ground on the other side, he sprang over the fence, lifted the corpse again, and quietly approached the edge of the quarry. He gave one glance down at the bottom, which was about seventy feet below him, and then cast the dead body from him. Down through the air it flew rapidly, and Fenwood heard the noise it made as it struck the ground beneath.

The sound died away, and was followed by a silence which, to Fenwood, was almost painful, so profound was it.

He stole back to the hedge very quietly, and got over it upon the road again. A strange feeling came over him. The prespiration broke out in big drops upon his forehead ; he felt sick at heart, and his knees shook beneath him. He thought he was going to fall to the ground, and with a dizzy head and confused mind clung to the railing of the fence for support—his face turned towards the quarry down which he had hurled his victim. He was standing thus, when he felt a hand laid upon his shoulder.

With a cry which almost resembled a scream, the guilty wretch turned round quickly. Standing near him was a tall, elderly man, with a stick in one hand and a basket in the other. Fenwood gave a scared look into the face so close to his own, and by the light of the moon saw that the eyes of the stranger were sightless.

" What are you doing here, my friend," said the pedlar —or it was he—" at this time of night ?"

Fenwood tried to speak, but he was so utterly confounded by the sudden and startling apparition that he could not utter a word.

"Silent!" said the blind man, in a very deliberate tone. "Are you dumb, or unwell? Which is it?"

"Who are you?" at last gasped Fenwood; "and what do you want?"

"Who am I!" replied the pedlar. "You don't know much about Cleator Moor, or else you would not have asked that question. My name is Charles Loftus, and I make my living by travelling and selling a few articles for common use. You can see that I am blind. As I was coming along the road to-night I fell over a stone, and injured myself so severely that I was obliged to creep through the hedge on the opposite side of the road into a field, where I have been lying for some time. However, I feel a grea-deal better now, although one of my legs still pains me very much; but I think I can manage to walk to White-haven, where I live. When I got out upon the road here I heard you breathing—the blind are usually very quick at hearing—and I came over to you. It would seem that you never heard me until I touched you with my hand."

"No," muttered Fenwood, "I did not hear you."

"I thought not," answered the pedlar. "But, I say, did you not hear a woman screaming a short time ago?"

The murderer grasped the rails of the fence beside him as he replied, in a trembling voice—

"I heard nothing of the kind."

"Humph!" muttered the blind man, speaking partly to himself. "It must have been my fancy then. And yet it seems strange. I thought, when I was lying in the field, that I heard a man and woman talking, and then the woman gave a scream which was checked suddenly. I tried to get up and go and see what was the matter, but I found I could not stand upon my feet. Have you been here long. ?"

" No," replied Fenwood, " I have not,"

" In which direction did you come ?"

" I came along the road from Whitehaven."

" And you heard nothing ?"

" Nothing."

" Then it is plain that I have been mistaken. Very likely the ugly tumble I got sent my wits a wool-gathering for the time. Judging by your voice, sir, I should say you are not a native of Cumberland."

" I am not," was the curt reply.

" I was sure of it," exclaimed the pedlar, " the first words I heard you speak. But I must leave you, for it must be late. What time do you think it is now ?"

" Between ten and eleven o'clock."

" Ah! It will be after midnight before I reach White-haven, for I am lame still. Good night to you !"

" Good night."

The blind man turned away, and Fenwood watched him as he went limping painfully along the road until he was lost to view. The strange and unexpected meeting with the pedlar at such a time had produced a very unpleasant impression upon the hardened ruffian; and it was with a sinking heart and a disturbed mind that he left the place near to which was lying the shattered body of his victim, and travelled with slow and unsteady steps over the Moor to his own house.

H

# CHAPTER X.

—o—

"Come back, come back," he cried in grief,
    Across the stormy water,
"And I'll forgive your Highland chief,
    My daughter, oh, my daughter!"
'Twas vain : the loud waves lash'd the shore,
    Return or aid preventing,
The waters wild went o'er his child,
    And he was left lamenting.—*Campbell.*

ETWEEN eleven and twelve o'clock òn the same night when the dreadful event described in the last chapter took place, Richard Somerville and his wife sat by the fire in the large kitchen of their dwelling, waiting very anxiously for the arrival of their daughter from Whitehaven. The servants had long since retired to rest, leaving the worthy couple alone. Both of them were uneasy and disturbed at the absence of Mary, and often did Mrs. Somerville, who was engaged in knitting, pause in her work and listen attentively, fancying that she heard the sound of approaching footsteps. But no such sound fell upon her ear, and with a sigh she resumed her labour.

The clock struck the hour of midnight, and then Mrs. Somerville rose from her seat, all the alarm which she felt showing itself in her face.

"Whativer can hev got Mary, Richard?" she said, in a trembling voice. "Theear's twelve o'clock struck, an' she isn't at heame yit. Does te' think owt can hev happen't till her?"

"Happen't!" said the farmer, with a face white to the very lips. "God bless me, woman, divn't talk that way, widoot thoo wants to send me daft. What can hev happen't till her?"

He spoke in an angry and impatient tone, which his wife had never heard him use before. She made no reply, but the tears rose to her eyes, and almost blinded her. Her husband saw the effect which his harshness had produced, and hastened to remove it.

"Nay," he said, tenderly, "thoo surely isn't seay simple as to start cryin' aboot a cross word! I didn't mean to say owt wrang, though I mebbe spok' rayder sharper than I should ha' dun; but for t' seake of aw that's gud say nowt agean aboot Mary meetin' wid any hurt. She's varra likely stopp't at Whitehebben that leate wid her friends that they didn't like to cum off heame to-neet, and seay they've meade it up to stay till mornin'. That's t' way on it noo, thoo may mak theesel' sure."

"Mebbe it is," said Mrs. Somerville, in a half-doubting tone.

"Mebbe!" sharply echoed the farmer; then checking himself, he proceeded, in a quiet and deliberate manner: "That's t' only way oot on it that I can see; seay, we'll tak oorsel's off to bed, and try to git a bit o' sleep. Mary 'll varra likely be here t' furst thing in t' mornin'."

With a sigh, his wife laid down her work, and proceeded with her husband upstairs to their bedroom.

Neither of them could sleep. The same feeling of dread and apprehension that some ill had befallen their daughter filled the minds of both, and when the day began to break both husband and wife arose and went down stairs.

Eight o'clock, nine o'clock came, and still no sign of Mary's appearance. When the latter hour struck, the farmer, who had been sitting for a long time moody and silent near the fire, rose hastily from his chair, and took up his hat and stick.

"I can stand this neay langer," he said, speaking very quickly. "I'll away ower to Abel Grayson's, and see if his dowter Ruth's got heame, an' if she hes, ax her if she knows owt o' Mary."

" Varra weel," said Mrs. Somerville. " I was just gahn to say that I thowt that was aboot t' best thing thoo could dui. And oh, Richard, for my seake, me lad, bide away neay langer nor thoo can help, but cum back till me suin an' tell me if thoo's heerd owt on her. Me lad, me lad, me heart's nearly brokken ! " And covering her face with her apron, the sorrowing mother wept like an infant.

"Whisht, woman, whisht!" said her husband, soothingly, although the tears stood in his own eyes. "Thoo's puttin' theesel' oot o' way widoot any 'ccasion. It 'll be reet annuff, I'se warrant. I'll cum back as suin as iver I can git."

He kissed his wife affectionately, and then left the house. Crossing the Moor at a rapid rate, he never halted until he stood in front of a large building called " The Knowe," which was the residence of Mr. Abel Grayson, a yeoman, and the father of the young lady with whom the reader has already been made acquainted. Richard Somerville knew the house well, and was about to enter it by the back way, but in crossing the yard leading to the rear of the premises, he met their owner face to face.

"Bless us aw weel, Dick," said Mr. Grayson, who was a big burly man, with a red face and loud voice, "is that thee? T' seet on the's gud for sore eyes, hooiver. Wor hes te' been this lang time, an' hoo is te' gitten on?"

"Middlin', Abel, only middlin'," replied the farmer. "But I've cum't on a lal bit o' business."

"What is it?" inquired Mr. Grayson. "But hedn't thoo better cum intil t' hoose an' sit down? We can talk just as weel sittin' as stannin'."

"I'll gang in in a minute, Abel," replied the farmer, "only I want the' to answer me a questin first."

"What is it?"

"Is thy dowter Ruth at heame?"

"To be sure she is."

"She was at Whitehebben yisterday?"

"Ay."

"When did she git back?"

"She got back last neet. What for?"

"Oh, Abel," said Richard, trembling in every limb, and wiping away the perspiration which stood in big drops upon his brow, "me an' oor oald woman's been sadly put oot o' t' way aboot oor Mary."

"Your Mary!" exclaimed Grayson, in amazement. "What aboot her?"

"She went to Whitehebben yisterday wid Ruth."

"I know she did."

"Well she hesn't cum't back yit."

"The deuce she hesn't!" cried Grayson. "Wey, Ruth got back suin efter ten o'clock, an' she said that her an' t' rest on them parted fray Mary at t' three road ends, and that Mary went reet forret towards heame."

"God be merciful to me!" said the farmer, staggering backwards. "Is this true?"

"True!" repeated Grayson. "Cum intil t' hoose, min, an' speak till Ruth hersel'."

The farmer, scarcely knowing what he was about, and walking like a man in a dream, complied with the request, and the two walked together into the room where Miss Grayson was seated.

"Good morning, Mr. Somerville," said the young woman, rising from her chair and approaching him. "How do you do, and how is Mary this morning? Good heavens! what is the matter?"

The last exclamation was caused by the ghastly look of the farmer, who, with a face as white as a sheet, staggered across the room to a chair, upon which he sat down, and nervously grasped the seat with both hands to save himself from falling to the ground.

"Tell her, Abel," he muttered, turning an imploring look upon Grayson. "Ax her aboot it, will te'? I cannot, I cannot!"

"Ruth, me lass," said Grayson, who was dreadfully shocked by the distress of his friend. "Richard here wants to know if his dowter Mary com wid the' and t' udder lasses fray Whitehebben last neet."

"Certainly she did," answered the young woman, with a look of astonishment.

"Wor did ye' leave her?"

"We parted from her at the end of the three roads, a short distance from Steadman's Quarry. But what are you asking these questions for?"

"Ruth," cried Richard Somerville, "we've niver seen Mary at heame sen she went away wid thee."

The young woman gasped for breath, and turned swiftly upon the farmer with a face as death-like as his own.

"What do you say?" she cried.

"I say," exclaimed the farmer, "that we've niver seen Mary sen she left heame yisterday; an' whativer can hev cum't on her is mair than I can tell. Her pooar mudder's fairly wild; and as for me—well, God help me, I feel as if I was takken leave o' me senses."

"Is it possible," murmured Ruth, pressing her hands tightly upon her breast, "that Mary cannot have gone home?" And then, with a frantic burst of grief, she cried out in piercing tones, "Oh, Mr. Somerville, what has become of her? where has she gone?"

"God only knows," answered the farmer. "I cannot tell."

"Neay," said Grayson, "an' thoo niver will tell if thoo sits here aw t' day. Cum, min, roose theesel, an' let's see if we can't find oot wor she is. I'll be bund, efter aw t' bodder thoo's givin' theesel', she's seafe annuff i' some snug corner. As like as nut thoo'll find her at heame when thoo gits back. But, anyway, let's be off till t' three road ends to begin wid. We'll start to luik for her wor Ruth and them parted wid her."

"Will you let me go with you, father?" said Ruth.

"No, me lass, I won't. Thoo's far better at heame," replied her father. "Thoo could dee neay gud, and thoo wad only be in t' road. Cum, Dick," he continued, addressing the farmer, "let's be off. Divn't fret in that way, min. I tell the' it's aw reet. We'll tak aw t' men we can find aboot t' spot wid us.'

The men servants, three in number, who where engaged in working close at hand, were called together, and the whole party at once set out for the place where, on the previous night, Mary had separated from her companions. As they proceeded along the road, several other young men—whom they met and made acquainted with the object of their journey—joined them.

"Here we are!" said Grayson, when they arrived at the end of the road branching off from the main one. "This is wor Ruth and her friends left Mary, and she wad gang on that way,' pointing with his finger to the right. "Noo, than, we'll gang t' seame way, an' see what we can mak oot."

The whole of the men proceeded cautiously along the road, Grayson leading the way. Richard Somerville appeared stupefied, and in all his movements seemed to obey a merely mechanical impulse. Grayson had not travelled many yards before he stopped suddenly, and the colour left his ruddy face as he looked at the ground.

"Theear seems to hev been a struggle of sum kind here," he muttered, "judgin' fray appearances. What's this?" he added, stooping down. "A woman's necklace! I say Dick, does te' know owt aboot this?"

"What is it?" cried the farmer, rushing eagerly forward. "A necklace! To be sure I know it. It's oor Mary's. Oh Abel," he continued, in a voice that was scarcely audible, so great was the emotion under which he laboured, "did I nut tell the' that summat hed happen't till her? Hoo did this cum here?"

"I can't tell that though," answered Grayson. "Things begins to luik varra queer; but keep up the' heart, Dick, we're mebbe frettin' oorsels aboot nowt. Let's gang a bit farder on."

The men again moved forward slowly, until they reached the fence which divided Steadman's Quarry from the road.

"She can't hev tummel't ower intil t' quarry," said Grayson; "it isn't possible. But we'd better luik ivery spot while we are aboot it. Here, yan or two o' you fellows, git ower t' dyke an' see if ye' see owt in t' quarry."

With a bound one of the men cleared the fence, and slowly creeping to the edge of the precipice, knelt down and gazed into the depths below. He looked but for a moment and then, with a cry of horror which pierced the heart of the almost frantic father like an arrow, he drew back.

"What the divil—Lord forgi'e me—is te' shootin' aboot, thoo clotheid?" said Grayson, angrily.

"Mr Grayson," said the man, in a low voice, as he approached the fence, "theear's a woman liggin' at t' bottom o' t' quarry, but whether it's Mary Sumerville or nut I can't say."

With a gasping sob the farmer dashed towards the fence, but the strong hand of Abel Grayson was laid upon his arm, and kept him back.

"Wor is te' gahn, Dick?" said the yeoman. "Bide wor thoo is; thoo can dui neay gud wid this wark. Be a man, min, for the wife's sake an' the own. Sum on ye' gang doon till t' bottom—ye' can easy git doon on t' udder side—an' see if theear's any truth in what Alick says."

In an instant half-a-dozen men leapt over the hedge, and passing round to the opposite portion of the quarry, descended to the ground below by a steep and winding path leading down the side. Some of them, amongst the rest Abel Grayson, remained behind; and the yeoman, striving hard to conceal his own agitation, did his utmost to console and soothe his friend.

The searchers were absent for a considerable time, but at last they could be seen from the road coming slowly up the rugged path, bearing amongst them the body of a woman. Sick at heart, the yeoman still maintained a firm grasp upon his friend, and eagerly watched the movements of the men, who were now slowly approaching the place where he stood. Not a word was spoken as the bearers, with terror depicted in their faces, came to the fence, and quietly laid their ghastly burden upon the ground.

No need for a second look at that countenance, distorted as it was by the death struggle, and at that form, almost every bone of which had been broken by the fall, to convince the agonised father that the body lying on the ground beside him was that of his only child. With a heart-rending cry, he shook off the hand which held him, and leaping over the fence, knelt down beside the corpse.

" Me bairn ! " he cried, in a broken voice ; " me bonny lass ! Mary, Mary, speak till the pooar oald fadder—to me that luiv'd the' far better than iver I luiv'd mesel'! Me darling," he continued, bending down and passionately kissing the cold lips of his daughter, " speak till me ! Oh, dear, she'll never speak till me agean ! I've lost her for iver—lost t' bonniest an' t' best lass that iver gladden'd an oald man's heart!"

The whole of the men around him were silently weeping like children. The sight of that dead body, so fearfully disfigured by violence, the grief of the bereaved father, had completely deprived them all of speech for the time being. Abel Grayson was the first to recover in part his composure.

"Theear's been foul play here," he said, breaking the silence. "She's been murder't afooar she was thrown doon t' quarry. Luik at t' marks on her throat."

"Ay," said a man standing beside him, "it's plain annuff that she hesn't cum't till her end be fair means. But whea wad hurt her? Neabody but a born divil; for she was yan o' t' finest young women we hed o' this country side."

The farmer still knelt by the corpse of his daughter, and whilst his sturdy frame shook from head to foot, he raised first one of her cold hands, then the other—at the same time imploring her to speak to him or his heart would break.

"Cum away, Dick," said Grayson, going over the fence to him, and endeavouring to lead him back to the road. "It's a terrible trial this; but thoo mun stand up agean it as weel as thoo can. The dowter's been murdered, min," added the yeoman, while his face darkened, "an' if thoo be t' man I tak the' for, thoo'll niver rist till thoo finds oot whea's to bleame for it. A curse leet on t' hoond that did such a deed!" continued Grayson, grinding his teeth together. "If I nobbet hed hold on him, I wad tear him limb fray limb."

"Mr. Grayson," cried one of the men from the road, "see ye', theear's a lot o' folk cummin' this way."

"An' seay theear is," said the yeoman, glancing along the highway at a large number of persons who were hurrying towards the quarry. "Hoo hev they got to know aboot this?"

"I think," replied the man, "Alick mun hev telt them. He went away fray here a lal bit sen."

"Like annuff," said Grayson. "But whea is this yung fellow that's cummin' up seay fast?"

In front of the rest was a young man, who bounded along the road with the speed of a greyhound. His face was as colourless as marble, and his eyes seemed to flash fire as, placing his hand lightly upon the railing, he cleared the fence and hurried to the place where Richard Somerville was still kneeling by the body of his daughter. The young man looked for a moment at the disfigured countenance, and then, with a groan, knelt down beside the farmer, who, roused by the sound, turned his eyes to the newcomer.

"Oh, James Blaylock, me dear lad," he cried, "is that thee? Me Mary, me own darlin' dowter! That," pointing to the corpse, "is aw that's left on her."

There was a moment's stillness, and then with a passionate energy, the young man spoke.

"Mr. Somerville," he said, "who has done this? Who is it that has murdered one of the best and noblest women that ever lived? Who has wrecked your happiness and mine for ever? Whose hand is it that has doomed me to walk the earth a miserable and blasted man? Mary," he continued, passing his arms round the corpse, and raising it tenderly from the ground, "my murdered darling, my wife, dear to me from the hour when I first saw you—if the giving of my own life would call back yours, I would give it freely; but, alas! it cannot be."

Some of the men approached him, but he motioned them away with his hand.

"Stand back, all of you!" he said, sternly. "No hands but my own and those of her father shall touch her now. By her side I will remain until the grave closes over her, and then the sooner I follow her the better."

He covered his face with his hands, and the hot, scalding tears sprang out from between his fingers. At last he looked at the farmer, who was kneeling beside him, and said, in a low, clear voice—

"Father, let us go home."

With a heavy sigh, the old man rose from the ground. James Blaylock did the same; and then, lifting up the body of her he had loved so well in life, he bore it to the fence.

"Will some of you help me over here with her?" he said, in a remarkably quiet tone. "That is all I wish you to do. I will bear her to her father's house myself."

The men gently relieved him of his sad load until he reached the road. They would have helped him to bear the body afterwards, but he resolutely declined their assistance, and, with his dead darling clasped close to his sorrowing heart, James Blaylock set out for the farm, followed by Richard Somerville and the rest of the persons who had assembled.

The farmer walked slowly along, with his eyes fixed upon the ground, becoming every moment more alive to the dreadful loss which he had met with—to the sad calamity which had befallen him. He prayed earnestly to his Maker to enable him to bear with resignation the terrible blow which had been struck by an unknown hand; but in the midst of his prayer he thought of the joy which his lost daughter had been to him and to her mother, and he felt that the chief tie which bound him to life had been taken away.

As he was silently walking along, a hand was laid upon his arm. He looked up, and saw Robert Fenwood standing near him, apparently very ill and agitated.

" Mr. Somerville," said the colliery manager, in a low voice, " this is a horrible story which I hear. Your daughter, they say, has been murdered. Is it true ?"

" It is," said the farmer. " God knows, it's only ower true ! Oh, Misther Fenwood, I'se nearly brokken-hearted !"

" And no wonder," said Fenwood, wiping away the perspiration from his face. " I never heard anything about it till within a few minutes ago. I have been very ill, as I dare say you have heard, and confined to my room for weeks till this morning. And it is the body of poor Mary that the young man walking before us is carrying in his arms ? What a dreadful business ! Let us hope that the man who has committed such a fearful crime will soon be found out and receive the punishment which he deserves. In the meantime, look to your Creator for strength to enable you to bear this great affliction. You know He tells us to call upon Him in the day of our trouble,

and He will deliver us ; and His promises are ever faith-
ful' ever sure.  I must leave you now; but in a day or two,
all well, I will call and see you.''

Robert Fenwood shook the hand of the farmer very
cordially, and then walked rapidly away.

# CHAPTER XI.

—o—

" That isle is now all desolate and bare,
    Its dwellings down, its tenants passed away ;
None but her own and father's grave is there,
    And nothing outward tells of human clay ;
You could not know where lies a thing so fair ;
    No stone is there to show, no tongue to say
What was : no dirge, except the hollow seas,
Mourns o'er the beauty of the Cyclades."—*Byron.*

WE will draw a veil over the scene which took place when Mrs. Somerville saw her beloved daughter taken into the house dead. There is something sacred in sorrow, and especially in the sorrow of a mother ; and it is not possible for the pen of a writer to describe the feelings which harrow the soul in the hour of affliction, and make the world seem a vast waste, uncheered by a single green spot. But those who know what it is to have lost a darling child, who have stood by the bed of death, and gazed in hopeless agony at the face, calm and immovable, until they felt tempted to exclaim, with Cowper—" Oh, that those lips had language !"—can form some conception of the impression made upon the stricken mother by the sight of the idol of her heart, who the day before had left home full of life and health, brought back cold and lifeless, without a single trace of her queenly beauty left.

James Blaylock insisted upon remaining in the same room beside the body of Mary. Nothing could induce him to change this determination. To the request that he would leave the house of mourning he made no answer, but sat quietly by the bed on which the young woman had been placed, his hand grasping hers, and his eyes fixed earnestly and tenderly upon the bruised and discoloured face.

The news of the dreadful occurrence spread with great rapidity over the district, and filled the minds of the people with horror and dismay. That a fearful crime had been committed was abundantly clear; and loud and deep were the execrations which were uttered on every hand against its unknown perpetrator. For Mary Somerville and her parents were widely known and generally esteemed by the rough and uncouth, but, in the main, kind-hearted people amongst whom they dwelt.

After the body had been conveyed to the farm-house, information of what had occurred was forwarded to the constable of Cleator. That worthy, on receipt of the intelligence, at once proceeded to the residence of Richard Somerville to investigate the facts for himself. The farmer and his wife were so completely prostrated by sorrow that they were unable to hold much conversation with him; but he obtained a few additional particulars from one of the servants, and then set out for Whitehaven to communicate with the authorities, and make arrangements with the Coroner for holding an inquiry as to the cause of death. After an absence of about four hours, the constable returned to the farm, and announced that the inquest had been fixed to take place at noon on the following day.

Meanwhile, the people of the district had not been idle. Steadman's Quarry, the place where the body had been

I

found, was visited shortly after the shocking discovery by a large number of persons, some of whom were attracted to it by idle curiosity, whilst others carefully examined the spot where the body was found, as well as the places around it, in the hope of finding some clue to the murderer. But the examination was fruitless, and as the evening drew on the people gave up the search in despair.

The place selected for holding the inquest was an inn near to the house of Richard Somerville, known as the Plough. The room chosen for this court of our Sovereign Lord the King was a parlour with a sanded stone floor, the furniture of which consisted of a large wooden settee, a few oak chairs, pictures, and a couple of spittoons placed on each side of the fire-grate. The apartment which was to be used for the solemn purpose of investigating a fearful crime had on the previous night been devoted to a very different purpose. Half-a-dozen men, crazy with drink, had fought a battle within its sacred precincts, and one of them had been driven with amazing swiftness across the floor to the window, through which his head had been sent by a terrific blow. Glaziers were not very plentiful at that time in the neighbourhood of Cleator Moor, and the landlady, in order to make the place fit to receive the Coroner and jury, had been under the necessity of covering the broken glass with paper.

As the hour approached when the inquiry was to commence, the jurymen began to arrive, and amongst the early comers was Robert Fenwood, who had been summoned by the constable to take part in the investigation. The face of the colliery manager when he entered the room was very pale, but he appeared quite calm and collected as he took his seat beside one of his brother jurors.

In front of the house a number of idlers had assembled, and were conversing together in whispers about the murder. But they became silent when they saw Richard Somerville, leaning on the arm of his friend Abel Grayson, coming toward the house, and a look of pity and sympathy rested on every face as the farmer passed through the small crowd.

The jurymen, witnesses, and constable had all reached the Plough, and were somewhat impatiently awaiting the arrival of Mr. Hayward, the Coroner for the district. They had not long to wait ; for a few minutes after twelve o'clock the gentleman referred to drove up to the door of the Plough in a gig. He was a tall, slender man, apparently between fifty and sixty years of age, and had the reputation of being a very shrewd and clever lawyer.

Stepping nimbly from the conveyance, he at once proceeded straight to the room where the jurymen were seated, and took his place at a table.

"Are all the jurymen here, constable?" said he, addressing the officer, who had followed him.

" I think so, sir," was the reply.

"Gentlemen," said Mr. Hayward, "please answer to your names as they are called."

As the name of each man was read out, he responded. When this was done, the Coroner cast a quick glance around the room, and said—

"Whom do you select for your foreman, gentlemen ?"

"Misther Fenwood, I should say," said a sturdy old farmer. "I think he's as likely for t' post as any on us."

" Stand up, gentlemen," said the Coroner, " and listen

to the oath taken by your foreman. For the oath which he is about to take is the same which you are to take yourselves."

The jurymen rose to their feet, and Mr. Hayward handed the Testament—that glorious record of the teachings and sufferings of the Saviour and his followers—to Fenwood. The murderer manifested no sign of emotion while the oath was administered to him, and when the Coroner ceased speaking, he touched the book with his lips, and quietly passed it to one of the men standing near him.

"Gentlemen," said Mr. Hayward, when the ceremony of swearing in the jury had been completed, "your duty is to inquire into the death of Mary Somerville. We will first of all go and view the body, and then return here and take the evidence."

The Coroner and jury, headed by the constable, then left the inn, and proceeded to the house of Richard Somerville. When they were shown into the room where the dead woman lay, the sight which they beheld was so painful that some of the strongest men present could not keep back their tears. The features of Mary were hardly recognisable, so bruised and disfigured were they; and few would have supposed, if they had not known her in life, that she had been one of the most handsome young women to be found on Cleator Moor, or for miles around it. By the side of the bed, upon a chair, sat James Blaylock. The poor fellow, jaded and worn out with watching, had fallen asleep, and his head was lying close to the face of the corpse, one of the hands of which he held firmly clasped in his own. To complete the melancholy picture,

Mrs. Somerville was kneeling at the bottom of the bed, with her face buried in the coverlet, weeping bitterly.

Neither Mrs. Somerville nor James Blaylock changed their position or stirred when the Coroner and jury entered the apartment. Despite his hardihood and wickedness, Fenwood shrank from looking at his victim, and it was only by summoning to his aid a bastard courage that he managed to overcome his reluctance. The change in the appearance of Mary Somerville was so great that it shocked even him for a moment, but the feeling quickly passed away, and gave place to one of satisfaction that there was not the slightest tittle of evidence to connect him with the murder, or the least suspicion that he had been concerned in it. He stood gazing earnestly for a short time at the dead woman, and, as he gazed, it seemed to him that a frown passed over the face. With a half-suppressed exclamation of affright, Fenwood turned away, and hurried out of the chamber after his companions.

When the Coroner and jury reached the inn again, the examination of the witnesses was commenced. Richard Somerville, in a broken voice, told how his daughter had left home on the day when she visited Whitehaven, as cheerful and light-hearted as he had ever known her to be on any previous occasion. Poor Ruth Grayson, who was almost distracted at the death of her companion, gave as coherent an account of all that took place up till the time when she and her companions parted from Mary, as her grief would permit. Mr. Grayson deposed to finding the necklace belonging to the young woman upon the road. The labourer who first saw the body at the bottom of the quarry, and two of the men who had assisted to bring it up, were also called as witnesses. This was the whole of the evidence.

" Well, gentlemen," said the Coroner, " it seems that at present we can get no further light thrown upon this case, and that, I think, is greatly to be deplored ; for there can be no doubt that this poor girl has been brutally and basely muidered. Who it is that has murdered her, or what motive any one could have for committing such an awful crime, is what we evidently cannot make out."

" Do ye' think she cuddent hev tummel't into t' quarry be accident ? " said a juryman.

" Nonsense, sir," said the Coroner. " How can you suppose that there could be any accident about an affair of this kind ? I tell you the girl has been murdered. What is that noise, constable ? " he continued, as he heard the sound of voices talking loudly at the door. " I wish you would keep the people quiet. Who is it ? "

" It's a man, sur," replied the constable, " that wants to cum in. He says he can give sum evidence."

" Very well," said the Coroner, " let him step this way."

The constable moved to one side, and the man to whom he had referred entered the apartment, and advanced with a firm and steady step to the table where Mr. Hayward was seated. Fenwood gave one look at him, and that look was sufficient to fill the mind of the colliery manager with dread, and blanch his face with terror. For in the witness he recognised the blind man who had conversed with him when he stood near to Steadman's Quarry after the commission of the murder. With a wildly-beating heart, Fenwood awaited the result of his examination.

" What is your name ? " said the Coroner.

" Charles Loftus," was the reply, delivered in a steady, calm tone.

" What are you ? "

" A hawker."

" You are blind, I see," said Mr. Hayward, with a touch of pity in his voice.

" I am, sir."

" Well, now, do you know anything about this ? "

" A little."

" Where do you live ? "

" At Whitehaven."

" Then did some one tell you about this inquest ? "

" I heard of the finding of the body in Steadman's Quarry, and that the inquest was to be. held here to-day ; so I have attended for the purpose of telling you all I know."

" Very well. Be good enough to do so, then in your own way."

In well chosen language, the pedlar proceeded to relate the particulars concerning the accident with which he had met, and which had compelled him to pause in his journey to Whitehaven, and closed by describing his interview with Fenwood, near to the quarry.

" You say," said the Coroner, when the witness had finished his statement, " that you thought you heard a shriek from a woman ? "

" I am sure, now, it was a woman shrieking," said the blind man, mournfully. " The man to whom I spoke denied that there had been any such sound, but he lied— and I am convinced that he murdered poor Miss Somer-

ville that night.   What was he doing there at that particular time ?"

" I want to ask you another question," said Mr. Hayward.   " Do you know this man of whom you speak ?"

The heart of Fenwood stood still as he leant forward,
waiting for the answer in breathless anxiety.

" I do not know him,' replied the blind man.

The murderer breathed freely again, and a smile passed
over his white face.

" You have no idea who he is ?" said the Coroner.

" Not the slightest," was the reply.

" Had you ever met him before ? "

" No."

" Then to you he was an entire stranger ?"

" He was."

" Well, gentlemen," said the Coroner, " we appear at
last to have got some evidence which tends to prove what
I have asserted—that this young woman came to her death
by unfair means ; but we seem to be as far as ever from
discovering the author of the crime.   I think, with the
witness, that the author was the man to whom he spoke
beside the quarry, but who that man is, is a mystery.
The witness, as you see, is blind, and cannot consequently
give us any description of the person with whom he conversed.   Do you wish to ask him any questions, gentlemen ?   Have you anything tc ask him, Mr. Fenwood ?"

" No, sir," replied Fenwood, with his Northumbrian
burr, " I have not.   He has given his evidence apparently
in a very straightforward manner."

With startling quickness, the blind man turned his
sightless eyes in the direction of the sound ; and with

equal rapidity Fenwood saw the terrible mistake which he had made by speaking in the presence of the witness. The words had scarcely died away, when the pedlar advanced across the room to where Fenwood was sitting, and laying his hand upon his shoulder, said, amid the most intense silence—

"This is the man to whom I spoke beside Steadman's Quarry on the night of the murder!"

Every man in the room, except Fenwood himself, sprang to his feet, and all eyes were turned towards the detected villain. His countenance assumed a sickly hue, his hands trembled, and his thin white lips quivered as he cast a terrified glance around the apartment. If any evidence of his guilt had been wanting, that evidence would have been furnished by his face. At last he slowly rose to his feet, and, like some wild animal at bay, looked defiantly at the company. He was standing so, when, with a loud cry, the farmer, who had remained in the room after giving his evidence, dashed forward, and seized him by the throat.

"Villain!" shouted Richard Somerville. "Thoo double-dyed, accursed villain! It's thee that's been t' cause of aw this, is it? It's thee that me and me wife hes to thenk for oor misery to-day! My dowter! My bonnie lass!" continued the almost maddened man, tightening his grasp upon the guilty wretch. "Give her back till me, or I'll choke the' wor thoo stands!"

The jurymen, who had been almost paralysed by the suddenness of the attack which had been made upon Fenwood, now interposed between the two men, and dragged the farmer back to a seat. The murderer, whose face was the colour of death, appeared to be scarcely conscious of what was going on, or to know that he had been attacked at all. Passing his hand over his brow, he looked with a vacant stare first at one frowning face and then another of the group of men by whom he was surrounded. Then with a cry which was neither a shriek nor a groan, but which partook of both, he fell heavily to the ground.

"He's tyan a fit," said one of the jurymen.

Mr. Hayward went up to the spot where Fenwood was lying, and looked long and earnestly into the face. The eyes were half-closed, and the lips were apart. The Coroner placed his hand upon the heart, and after allowing it to rest there for a short time, he turned away.

"What ails him?" inquired the man who had spoken last.

"In the sense in which you mean it," replied the Coroner, "he ails nothing, for he is dead. Come, gentlemen," he continued, "don't look so frightened. However bad the man was in life, he cannot harm you now. Tell the people to remove the body out of the room, and then we will proceed with the inquiry."

The corpse was immediately taken into another apartment, and shortly afterwards it was conveyed to the house which had been the home, when living, of him who had been struck down in the hour of his fancied security, and had passed in a moment from the judgment of this world to that tribunal which is presided over by an all-wise God.

The Coroner, after his instructions had been carried out, proceeded to sum up the evidence, and the jury, without hesitation, returned a verdict of "Wilful Murder against Robert Fenwood."

\*        \*        \*        \*        \*

\*        \*        \*        \*        \*

With the death of Fenwood our story ends, and it is simply necessary to add a few words in conclusion concerning some of the humble characters who have taken part in it.

Two funerals took place at Cleator Moor upon the same day. One was that of Mary Somerville, whose remains were followed to their last resting place by a large number of persons, anxious to testify in this way their sympathy with and respect for her parents, and their sorrow for her untimely end. The other was that of her murderer, who was so universally condemned and hated, that it was with difficulty the necessary number of bearers could be found to carry him to the grave. The only regret of the people in connexion with him appeared to be that by his sudden death he had cheated the gallows.

Shortly after the burial of his sweetheart, James Blaylock left Cleator Moor for another and a distant part of the country. His friends tried to persuade him to remain, but their efforts were of no avail. The place was hateful to him, and he longed to get away from it. But he never forgot Mary Somerville, and many a time in after years his memory wandered back with regret and sorrow to that memorable night when she promised to be his wife.

Mr. Jenkins, who has from time to time made the reader acquainted with the hardships and persecution to which he was subjected by the youths of Cleator Moor, was ultimately compelled to seek a refuge from his misery in

Whitehaven. But he only stepped out of the frying pan into the fire. His fame had preceded him, and on the first night of his stay in Whitehaven the unfortunate man was under the necessity of engaging in a hand-to-hand fight with about twenty lads, who thought proper to honour him and Mrs. Jenkins with a visit.

Shortly after the inquest the health of Charles Loftus began to decline, and he ceased to visit the villages around Whitehaven as usual. But for several years after his death, the testimony of The Hidden Witness—which led to the detection of the perpetrator of a horrible crime—formed the subject of many a conversation amongst the people of Cleator Moor and the villages adjoining during the long winter nights.

And what of the farmer and his wife ? Well, it is scarcely necessary to say that they never properly recovered from the shock caused by the death of their daughter. But Time kindly mitigated the great sorrow of their lives, and as the months rolled by the aged couple began to think and speak of their darling as they would have done of an angel in heaven. So resigned did he become that about a year after the death of Mary, the farmer had a tombstone placed over her grave, recording her name, the year in which she was born, and that in which she died, and inscribed with that sentence so expressive of submission to the will of our Heavenly Father—" The Lord gave, and the Lord hath taken away ; blessed be the name of the Lord."

THE END.

I. EVENING, PRINTER, COCKERMOUTH.